Terry Pratchett was born in 1948 and is still not dead. He started work as a journalist one day in 1965 and saw his first corpse three hours later, work experience *meaning* something in those days. After doing just about every job it's possible to do in provincial journalism, except of course covering Saturday afternoon football, he joined the Central Electricity Generating Board and became press officer for four nuclear power stations. He'd write a book about his experiences if he thought anyone would believe it.

All this came to an end in 1987 when it became obvious that the Discworld series was much more enjoyable than real work. Since then the books have reached double figures and have a regular place in the bestseller lists. He also writes books for younger readers. Occasionally he gets accused of literature.

Terry Pratchett lives in Wiltshire with his wife Lyn and daughter Rhianna. He says writing is the most fun anyone can have by themselves.

Stephen Briggs was born in Oxford in 1951 and he still lives there, with his wife Ginny and their sons, Philip and Christopher.

In what would generally pass for real life he works for a small government department dealing with the food industry. However, as an escape to a greater reality, he has been involved for many years in the machiavellian world of amateur dramatics, which is how he came to discover the Discworld.

Stephen is, by nature, a Luddite, but the Discworld has drawn him into the world of PCs, wordprocessing and electronic mail; he has even been known to paddle on the Internet. His other interests include sketching, back-garden ornithology and Christmas. He has never read *Lord of the Rings* all the way through.

GOOD OMENS (with Neil Gaiman)
STRATA
THE DARK SIDE OF THE SUN

TRUCKERS*
DIGGERS*
WINGS*
THE CARPET PEOPLE
ONLY YOU CAN SAVE MANKIND*
JOHNNY AND THE DEAD*
JOHNNY AND THE BOMB*

*also available in audio

and published by Corgi

THE UNADULTERATED CAT
MORT: A DISCWORLD BIG COMIC
THE DISCWORLD COMPANION
(with Stephen Briggs)
TERRY PRATCHETT'S
DISCWORLD QUIZBOOK
by David Langford

published by Gollancz

TERRY PRATCHETT'S

MORT
the play

adapted for the stage by
STEPHEN BRIGGS

CORGI BOOKS

MORT – THE PLAY
A CORGI BOOK : 0 552 14429 0

First publication in Great Britain

PRINTING HISTORY
Corgi edition published 1996

Mort originally published in Great Britain by
Victor Gollancz Ltd in association with Colin Smythe Ltd
Copyright © Terry Pratchett 1987

Stage adaptation copyright © by
Terry Pratchett and Stephen Briggs 1996

Discworld® is a registered trademark

Set in 12pt Monotype Ehrhardt by
Phoenix Typesetting, Ilkley, West Yorkshire

Corgi Books are published by Transworld Publishers Ltd,
61–63 Uxbridge Road, London W5 5SA,
in Australia by Transworld Publishers (Australia) Pty Ltd,
15–25 Helles Avenue, Moorebank, NSW 2170,
and in New Zealand by Transworld Publishers (NZ) Ltd,
3 William Pickering Drive, Albany, Auckland.

Reproduced, printed and bound in Great Britain by
Cox & Wyman Ltd, Reading, Berks.

INTRODUCTION

AN AWFULLY BIG ADVENTURE

Since the publication of *The Streets of Ankh-Morpork*, I have been drawn ever further into the Discworld universe. As well as working with Terry on *The Discworld Companion*, I was suddenly in demand – well, OK, I was in demand when I was dressed as *Death* – to pose for publicity photos. The first session was for a Discworld computer game; then Death was again summoned to be photographed with Dave Greenslade and Terry for his CD *From the Discworld*. I was delighted to find myself invited to 'play' Didactylos in the *Small Gods* track; yes, that was me – 'Nevertheless, the Turtle *does* move'. Er . . . not my *real* voice, of course.

Death even got an invitation to London's flashiest Indian restaurant to have a curry with a group of journalists as part of the publicity for a Discworld computer game. A whole room full of journalists but, unfortunately for Death, no take-away.

My drama club has now staged *Wyrd Sisters*, *Mort*, *Guards! Guards!*, *Men at Arms* and *Maskerade*. We were even invited to act out a tiny extract from 'our' *Guards!*

Guards! for Sky TV's Book Programme.

In fact, Oxford's Studio Theatre Club were the first people ever to dramatise the Discworld.

We had a theatre that seats ninety people. We had a stage that was about the size of a pocket handkerchief with the wings of Tinkerbell. Put on a Discworld play? Simple . . .

A flat, circular world borne through space on the backs of four enormous elephants who themselves stand on the carapace of a cosmically large turtle? Nothing to it. A seven-foot skeleton with glowing blue eyes? *No* problem. A sixty-foot fire-breathing dragon? A cinch.

My drama club had already staged its own adaptations of other works: Monty Python's *Life of Brian* and *Holy Grail* – and Tom Sharpe's *Porterhouse Blue* and *Blott on the Landscape*. We were looking for something new when someone said, 'Try Terry Pratchett – you'll like him.'

So I ventured into the previously uncharted territory of the 'Fantasy' section of the local bookstore. I read a Terry Pratchett book; I liked it. I read all of them. I wrote to Terry and asked if we could stage *Wyrd Sisters*. He said yes.

Wyrd Sisters sold out.

So did *Mort* the year after.

So did *Guards! Guards!*, *Men at Arms* and *Maskerade* in the three years after that. In fact, 'sold out' is too modest a word. 'Oversold very quickly so that by the time the local newspaper mentioned it was on we'd had to close the booking office' is nearer the mark.

My casts were all happy enough to read whichever book we were staging, and to read others in the canon too. The books stand on their own, but some knowledge of the wider Discworld ethos helps when adapting the stories, and can help the actors with their characterisations.

The Discworld stories are remarkably flexible in their character requirements. *Mort* has been performed successfully with a cast of three (adding in an extra thrill for the audience, who knew that sooner or later a character would have to have a dialogue with *themselves*. But it turned out very well). On the other hand, there is plenty of scope for peasants, wizards, beggars, thieves and general rhubarb merchants if the director is lucky enough to have actors available.

I'd better add a note of caution here. There are a lot of small parts in the plays which nevertheless require good acting ability (as we say in the Studio Theatre Club: 'There are no small parts, only small actors'). The character may have only four lines to say but one of them might well be the (potentially) funniest line in the play. Terry Pratchett is remarkably democratic in this respect. Spear-carriers, demons and even a humble doorknocker all get their moment of glory. Don't let them throw it away!

Terry writes very good dialogue. Not all authors do. But Terry, like Dickens, writes stuff which you can lift straight into your play. Although it was often necessary to combine several scenes from the book into one scene in the play, I tried to avoid changing the original Pratchett dialogue. After all, you perform an author's work because you like their style; as much of that style as possible should be evident in the play.

We aimed to keep our adaptations down to about two hours running time – with a 7.30 start and allowing 20 minutes for an interval, that would get the audience into the pub for an after-play drink by about 9.50, with the cast about 10 minutes after them (although slower-moving members of the audience could find the cast already there propping up the bar – we are true Coarse Actors!). Also, two hours is about right for the average play. This of course meant that some difficult decisions had to be taken in order to boil down the prose.

The important thing was to decide what was the basic plot: anything which didn't contribute to that was liable to be dropped in order to keep the play flowing. Favourite scenes, even favourite characters, had to be dumped.

I had to remember that not all the audience would be dyed-in-the-wool Pratchett fans. Some of them might just be normal theatre-goers who'd never read a fantasy novel in their whole lives, although I have to say that these now are a dwindling minority.

The books are episodic, and this can be a difficult concept to incorporate into a play. Set changes slow down the action. Any scene change that takes more than 30 seconds means you've lost the audience. Even *ten*-second changes, if repeated often enough, will lead to loss of interest.

The golden rule is – if you can do it without scenery, do it without scenery. It's a concept that has served radio drama very well (everyone *knows* that radio has the best scenery). And Shakespeare managed very well without it, too.

The plays do, however, call for some unusual props. Many of these were made by the cast and crew: a door with a hole for a talking, golden doorknocker, coronation mugs, large hourglasses for Death's house, sponge chips and pizzas, shadow puppets, archaic rifles, dragon-scorched books and Discworld newspapers ('Patrician Launches Victim's Charter'). Other, more specialised props were put 'out to contract': Death's sword and scythe, an orang-utan, the City Watch badge, a Death of Rats, a Greebo and two swamp dragons (one an elaborate hand puppet and one with a fire-proof compartment in its bottom for a flight scene).

Since the Studio Theatre Club started the trend in 1991, Terry and I have had many enquiries about staging the books – from as far afield as California, South Africa, New Zealand and Australia (as well as Sheffield, Glastonbury and the Isle of Man).

So how did our productions actually go? We enjoyed them. Our audiences seemed to enjoy them (after all, some of them were prepared, year after year, to travel down to Abingdon in Oxfordshire from as far afield as Taunton, Newcastle upon Tyne, Ipswich, Basingstoke and . . . well, Oxford). Terry seemed to enjoy them, too. He said that many of our members looked as though they had been recruited straight off the streets of Ankh-Morpork. He said that several of them were born to play the 'rude mechanicals' in Vitoller's troupe in *Wyrd Sisters*. He said that in his mind's eye the famous Ankh-Morpork City Watch *are* the players of the Studio Theatre Club.

I'm sure these were meant to be compliments.

MORT

We staged *Mort* in 1992, after a surprising (to us) success with *Wyrd Sisters* the previous year.

As with *Wyrd Sisters*, some difficult choices had to made to reduce Terry's book into a two-hour play, and a number of favoured scenes had to go (including the scene in the inn where the reality interface passes through while Mort drinks scumble). Inevitably, the adaptation was written originally with the restrictions of the tiny Unicorn Theatre, and the numbers of players I'd have available, in mind. This meant that complicated scenic effects were virtually impossible. Anyone thinking of staging a Discworld play can be as imaginitive as they like – call upon the might of Industrial Light & Magic, if it's within their budget. But they *can* be staged with fairly achievable effects, and the notes that accompany the text are intended to be a guide for those with limited or no budget. Bigger groups, with teams of experts on hand, can let their imaginations run wild!

The script as it appears here is now tried and tested, but it isn't the *only* way to adapt the book. Other groups have made different choices. Some have many more people available than we did, and they've looked to add in 'crowd' scenes – perhaps the Duke's Head/Queen's Head scene, build up the Unseen University scenes and readmit the Librarian. Others have chosen to drop almost all the 'narration' bits. What is important, though, is to ensure that a scene left in at one point in the play doesn't rely for part of its humour or logic on a scene you've cut elsewhere – or that a scene you've added as a show-stopper doesn't end up just slowing it down instead!

In short, though, our experience and that of other groups is that it pays to work hard on getting the costumes and lighting right, and to keep the scenery to little more than, perhaps, a few changes of level. One group with some resourceful technophiles achieved magnificent 'scenery' simply with sound effects and lighting ('dripping water' and rippling green light for a dungeon scene, for example). There's room for all sorts of ideas here. The Discworld, as it says in the books, is your mollusc.

Characterisation

Within the constraints of what is known and vital about each character, there is still room for flexibility of interpretation. With the main roles, though, you have to recognize that your audiences will expect them to look as much like the book descriptions as possible. However, most drama clubs don't have a vast range from which to choose and it's the acting that's more important than the look of the player when it comes down to it!

Death. On the Discworld he is a seven-foot tall skeleton of polished bone, in whose eye sockets there are tiny points of light (usually blue). He normally wears a robe apparently woven of absolute darkness – and sometimes also a riding cloak fastened with a silver brooch. He smells, not unpleasantly, of the air in old, forgotten rooms.

His scythe looks normal enough, except for the blade: it is so thin you can see through it, a pale blue shimmer that could slice flame and chop sound. The sword has the same ice-blue, shadow-thin blade, of the extreme thinness necessary to separate body from soul.

His horse, though pale as per traditional specification, is entirely alive and called Binky. Death once tried a skeleton horse after seeing a woodcut of himself on one – Death is easily influenced by that sort of thing – but he had to keep stopping to wire bits back on. The fiery steed that he tried next used to set fire to the stables.

Despite rumour he is not cruel. He is just terribly, terribly good at his job. It is said that he doesn't get angry, because anger is an emotion, and for emotion you need glands; however, he does seem to be capable of a piece of intellectual disapproval which has a very similar effect.

He is a traditionalist who prides himself on his personal service, and can become depressed when this is not appreciated.

Death has a property not locatable on any normal atlas, on which he has called into being a house and garden. There are no colours there except black, white and shades of grey; Death could use others but fails to see their significance. And, because he almost by definition lacks true creative ability – he can only copy what he has seen – no real time passes in his domain.

There is a strong suggestion in the books that Death is somehow *on our side*.

To stage Death, even *we* had to decide to spend some money. Death, we recognised, is the pivotal character; you *have* to get him as right as you can! We had Death's head-mask and gloves, robes and weapons made for us to our design by a firm called Creative Madness (now run as Spyder's FX, Chapel Corner, Exeter Road, Winkleigh, Devon). His eyes glowed blue, and the clear perspex blades of his sword and scythe – 'sharp' enough to see through! – had a tiny blue light hidden in their handles so that, on a dimly-lit stage, they glowed eerily. To aid this, we made sure that whenever Death or Mort used their weapons the stage was lit only by a strobe and the action changed to slow-motion; this enhanced the magical happening as Death took people and ensured that the glowing sword and scythe were shown to their best effect.

To get our Death as close as we could to his seven-foot height, we had him stalking around on heavy, stacked-up ice-skating boots. The final effect was very impressive and has not only made guest appearances in our subsequent Discworld plays, but has also featured in publicity shots for the Dave Greenslade *From the Discworld* CD and for the Psygnosis *Discworld* computer game.

Mort. Mortimer. Youngest son of Lezek. Tall, red-haired and freckled, thin white face, with the sort of body that seemed to be only marginally under its owner's control; it appeared to have been built out of knees. He had the kind of vague, cheerful helpfulness that serious men soon learned to dread.

Despite these drawbacks Mort was chosen by Death to be his apprentice, and during that time became considerably less undirected and considerably more serious. Mort married Ysabell and became Duke of Sto Helit.

As Duke, his coat of arms was a faux croisé on a sablier rampant against a sable field. His motto: NON TIMETIS MESSOR.

Ysabell. Death's adopted daughter. When first introduced, she was a sixteen-year-old young woman (although the age can be changed if you don't have a suitable actress!) with silver hair, silver eyes and a slight suggestion of too many chocolates. Not, of course, a blood relation to the Grim Reaper – no real explanation has been given as to why he saved her as a baby when her parents were killed in the Great Nef.

It says a lot for Ysabell's basic mental stability that she remained even halfway sane in Death's house, where no time passes and black is considered the appropriate colour for almost everything. She certainly developed an obsessive interest in tragic heroines and also a fixation for the colour pink.

Albert. Death's manservant, but also Alberto Malich the Wise, the founder of the Unseen University (1222–1289 by the city count of that time).

Although he is, in real years, only about 67, he has been alive while two thousand years have passed on the Disc.

The generally held belief is that Alberto, one of the most powerful wizards alive at the time, tried to outwit Death by performing the Rite of AshkEnte backwards. In so far as his charred notebooks hold any clue, he seemed to believe that he could obtain another 67 years of life.

Back on the Disc, Albert would have had only 91 days, 3 hours and 5 minutes left to live. That is now down to a handful of seconds, since most of it has been frittered away on shopping trips and holidays back in the world. When in Ankh-Morpork, Albert stays at the Young-Men's-Reformed-Cultists-of-the-Ichor-God-Bel-Shamharoth Association, where he nicks the soap and towels (Death has not got the knack of making towels, or soap, or anything to do with plumbing).

In appearance, Albert is a small hunched old man. This merely shows that first impressions can be wrong. Second impressions suggest quite a tall, wiry man who merely walks like the third illustration along in the usual How Man Evolved diagram. He has a red nose which drips so much that people talking to him blow their own noses out of sympathy.

Cutwell. Wizard in Wall Street, Sto Lat. Cutwell is a young wizard, 20 years old, with curly hair and no beard. He is basically good-humoured, with a round, rather plump face – pink and white like a pork pie. When first seen in the book he was wearing a grubby hooded robe with frayed edges and a pointy hat which has seen better days.

He lodged in a very untidy house with peeling plaster, and a blackened brass plaque by the door – 'Igneous Cutwell, DM (Unseen), Marster of the Infinit, Illluminartus, Wyzard to Princes, Gardian of the Sacred Portalls, If Out leave Maile with Mrs Nugent Next Door'.

The room inside combined the usual get-it-in-a-kit wizard's workroom, down to the stuffed alligator and things in jars, with the typical room of a student (that is to say, there are no longer any recognisable flat surfaces and the carpet parts company with the sole of the foot only with reluctance).

Keli. Princess Kelirehenna of Sto Lat. When we first encountered her, she was a slim, red-haired girl of fifteen (mind you, drama clubs have used much older actresses to good effect) with a strong jawline; not beautiful, being over-endowed in the freckle department and, frankly, rather on the skinny side.

Her role in life was to fail to be killed by an assassin due to the gland-led incompetence of Mort.

She eventually became Her Supreme Majesty, Queen Kelirehenna I, Lord of Sto Lat, Protector of the Eight Protectorates, and Empress of the Long Thin Debated Piece Hubwards of Sto Kerrig.

Costumes

We played most of the characters around the Renaissance period, although Ysabell was dressed in pre-Raphaelite style (apart from the pink fluffy dressing-gown), Albert was a Georgian manservant, and Keeble was somewhere around the twentieth century. Cutwell's long, green, medieval robe was set off with a college scarf (not the real

UU one – they've only become available since then!); he also sported horn-rimmed specs repaired 'Jack-Duckworth-style' with sticking plaster. Mort wore a wild-looking red wig, and our Princess Keli coloured her own hair a rather more tasteful red, to suit the book description.

Scenery

Virtually none. We performed on a black set decorated with hourglasses and books and dominated by an 'oil painting' of Alberto Malich. Within that we used the minimum of furniture necessary to establish the settings. Above the stage was our screen for the shadow puppets.

Special effects

Apart from Death's glowing scythe and sword, we also used flash pods for Death's entrance and exit from the Rite of AshkEnte scene and strobes for those occasions when the sword or scythe were wielded. Other little bits and pieces included:

Albert's runny nose. Our budget was tiny for this aspect. We managed to run to a false hooked nose for Albert, Death's manservant, and a search of haberdasher's unearthed an opalescent teardrop bead that we stitched loosely to the tip of the nose, where it trembled most realistically!

Binky. Binky gave us more worries. A panto horse would look ridiculous; so would a stuffed head appearing from the wings. Should we simply ignore this aspect of the plot? No! We decided on a series of shadow puppets, operated against a painted screen above the stage. In the event this simple device not only got over the concept of the flying horse but also, with carefully selected musical accompaniment, entertained the audience during the occasional brief bit of scene-changing.

The Dead. The other concern was the need for people to die on stage; for there to be a body, but for the same character to be able still to walk about and talk to Death or Mort. We decided on a bit of cracker-barrel symbolism: the person, on the point of death (in the strobe light), would cast off some heavy outer garment, which would then become their 'body' for the living people on stage. The actor was then free to become their own late spirit.

The Doorknocker. Our doorknocker had his head thrust through a hole in Cutwell's door. He was painted with gold make-up and gripped a plastic ring in his mouth. He rehearsed with a Biro gripped in his teeth in order to get used to enunciating clearly through this encumbrance!

The Librarian. Er . . . we fudged this one. Cut him out completely. Decided he wasn't worth the expense, as he is only a minor character in this play and isn't essential for plot advancement. (We made it up to him the following year in *Guards! Guards!*)

However, if you *do* decide that he's indispensible, you might like to know that the Orangutan Foundation do now have an orangutan costume that they may be prepared to loan to a careful user – subject to its being returned in at least as good a condition as that in which it went out, and to a donation for their organisation. They can be contacted via Ashley Leiman, Orangutan Foundation, 7 Kent Terrace, London, NW1 4RP (Tel/Fax: 0171 724 2912).

Stephen Briggs
May 1996

TERRY PRATCHETT'S
MORT

adapted for the stage by Stephen Briggs

CAST OF CHARACTERS

Death: *an anthropomorphic personification*
Mort: *a youth*
Lezek: *Mort's father*
Ysabell: *Death's daughter*
Albert: *Death's servant*
King Olerve
Duke of Sto Helit
Princess Keli
Cutwell: *a wizard*
Towncrier
Doorknocker
Goodie Hamstring: *a witch*
Abbott Lobsang
Assassin
Maid
Woman in street
Mr Keeble: *a clerk*
High Priest
Rincewind: *a wizard*
Bursar: *of Unseen University*
Agatean Prince
Agatean Vizier
High Priest
Acolyte
M.C.
Guests, Wizards, Guards, etc.

Play first performed by the Studio Theatre Club
at the Unicorn Theatre, Abingdon
on 10 to 13 June 1992

SCENE 1 – A STREET IN SHEEPRIDGE

(On stage are MORT, LEZEK, plus WALTER and his equally unprepossessing MUM. All stand looking rather bored. LEZEK turns to address the audience) [NOTE – as a device to keep the play moving, we used various members of the cast as 'narrators', with them stepping out of the action to address the audience, in character, directly]

LEZEK
 This is the hiring fair at Sheepridge. On Discworld. Not a spherical world like yours, but flat. Like a pizza; no anchovies, though. Discworld moves through space on the backs of four gigantic elephants. They in turn stand on the back of a colossal turtle – the Great A'Tuin. Just goes to show, the gods do have a sense of humour! *(pause)* People bring their children to the hiring fair to try to get them apprenticed off to a good trade. That's my son Mort. The fair closes at midnight; we've been here all day, but no-one wanted Mort. Again.

(HRITA enters)

HRITA
 Hello, Lezek. Happy Hogswatch Night. Here again with young Mort I see. How many years is it now?

3

LEZEK
Don't ask. Sometimes I think I'll never apprentice him off.

(MORT crashes into a trader, knocking his wares onto the ground)

HRITA
He's an awkward bugger, isn't he?

LEZEK
His heart's in the right place, mind.

HRITA
Ah. 'Course, 'tis the rest of him that isn't.

LEZEK
I did hear you'd got a place at your farm, Hrita.

HRITA *(hurriedly)*
Ah. Got an apprentice in, didn't I?

LEZEK
Ah. When was that?

HRITA
Yesterday. All signed and sealed. Sorry. Look, I got nothing against your Mort, see, he's as nice a boy as you could wish to meet. It's just that . . .

4

LEZEK

I know, I know. He couldn't find his bum with both hands.

(HRITA wanders off, looking relieved. LEZEK turns to the audience)

There's only us and Walter the half-wit left. And it's almost midnight.

(Enter CYRUS, the Cesspit cleaner)

LEZEK

Thank God. Here's Cyrus, the cesspit cleaner. Cyrus, hello, how's the business going?

(CYRUS nods, then walks round MORT and WALTER, thoughtfully, before finally selecting WALTER, and exiting with him and his MUM)

Well, that's that. Another bloody year gone.

MORT

Are you sure this tunic's all right, Dad?

LEZEK

Very nice. For the money.

MORT

It itches. I think there's things in here with me.

LEZEK

There's many a lad would be only too glad of a nice, warm, er . . . garment, like that.

(pause)

MORT

Dad, why does the sun come out during the day, instead of at night when the light would be more useful?

LEZEK

What? For goodness' sake, Mort, how should I know? Your trouble is you think too much.

(Midnight starts to chime)

Well, that's it, midnight. We'd better find somewhere to sleep. I'm afraid no-one's going to employ you, Mort.

MORT

It's not midnight 'til the last stroke.

(They hear the noise of hooves, clip-clopping nearer. The lights darken. DEATH enters. [NOTE – actually, we 'revealed' him instead, to get better dramatic impact. At the appropriate moment there were crashing chords of organ music and the curtains opened to reveal DEATH with his back to the audience; he turned slowly as the music played and then moved downstage to MORT and LEZEK] He raises his hand and the clock stops chiming. LEZEK freezes)

DEATH
WHAT IS YOUR NAME, BOY?

MORT
Uh . . . Mortimer, sir. They call me Mort.

DEATH
WHAT A COINCIDENCE.

MORT *(nervously)*
Excuse me, sir, but are you Death?

DEATH
CORRECT. FULL MARKS FOR OBSERVATION, THAT BOY.

MORT
My father is a good man. I don't know what you've done to him, but I'd like you to stop it. No offence meant.

DEATH
I HAVE MERELY PUT US OUTSIDE TIME FOR A MOMENT. HE WILL SEE AND HEAR NOTHING THAT DISTURBS HIM. NO, BOY, IT IS YOU I CAME FOR.

MORT
Me?

DEATH
YOU ARE HERE SEEKING EMPLOYMENT?

MORT
    You're looking for an apprentice?

DEATH
    OF COURSE.

*(DEATH waves a hand. The clock chimes continue. LEZEK
unfreezes. He blinks)*

LEZEK
    Didn't see you there for a moment. Sorry – mind must
    have been elsewhere.

DEATH
    I WAS OFFERING YOUR BOY A POSITION.
    I TRUST THAT MEETS WITH YOUR
    APPROVAL?

LEZEK
    What was your job again?

DEATH
    I USHER SOULS INTO THE NEXT WORLD.

LEZEK
    Of course. Sorry, should have guessed from the clothes.
    Very necessary work, very steady. Established business?

DEATH
    I HAVE BEEN GOING FOR SOME TIME, NOW,
    YES.

LEZEK
  Fair enough. Well, I . . :

MORT *(tugging at his sleeve)*
  Dad . . .

DEATH
  WHAT YOUR FATHER SEES AND HEARS IS
  NOT WHAT YOU SEE AND HEAR. DO NOT
  WORRY HIM. DO YOU THINK HE WOULD
  WANT TO SEE ME – IN THE FLESH, AS IT
  WERE?

MORT
  But you're Death! You go around killing people!

DEATH *(offended)*
  I? KILL? CERTAINLY NOT. PEOPLE KILL
  PEOPLE. DISEASE KILLS PEOPLE. I TAKE
  OVER FROM THEN ON. AFTER ALL, IT'D BE A
  BLOODY STUPID WORLD IF PEOPLE GOT
  KILLED WITHOUT DYING, WOULDN'T IT?

MORT
  Well, yes . . . OK, if Father says it's all right.

(He turns to his father)

LEZEK
  How do you feel about this, Mort? It's not everyone's
  idea of an occupation, undertaking.

MORT
Undertaking?

(DEATH nods and puts a conspiratorial finger to where his lips would have been)

It's very interesting. I think I'd like to try it.

LEZEK *(indicating MORT)*
He's a good lad at heart. A bit dreamy, that's all. I suppose we were all young once.

DEATH
NO. I DON'T THINK SO.

LEZEK *(to MORT)*
I hope you'll be able to drop in and see us soon.

MORT
I'm not sure that would be a good idea. I'll try and write you a letter.

LEZEK
There's bound to be someone passing who can read it to us. Goodbye, Mort.

(They embrace. LEZEK starts to leave)

MORT
Goodbye, Dad.

(LEZEK exits)

DEATH *(taking some coins from a purse)*
HERE, BOY. SOME MONEY.

MORT
What for?

DEATH
TO BUY YOU SOME NEW CLOTHES.

MORT
These were new today. Yesterday, I mean.

DEATH
IT CERTAINLY ADDS A NEW TERROR TO POVERTY.

MORT *(looking at the coins)*
Here, these are from all over the Disc. How did you come by them all?

DEATH *(putting a finger to his eyes)*
IN PAIRS.

(MORT considers this. They exit. As we see them fly over on Binky, we hear Death's voice over the speakers)

THERE IT IS, BOY, OUR TERRITORY. FROM CORI CELESTI TO THE CIRCLE SEA. FROM KLATCH TO THE RAMTOPS. MAGNIFICENT. *(pause)* I DON'T KNOW ABOUT YOU, BOY, BUT I COULD MURDER A CURRY.

(Lights black out)

SCENE 2 – DEATH'S STUDY

(Next morning. There is a desk and chair. The desk and walls are covered in large books and hourglasses. MORT enters and looks warily about him. After a moment YSABELL enters. She creeps up behind him and pinches him on the arm)

MORT
Ow!

YSABELL
Hmm. So you're really real. What's your name, boy?

MORT
Mortimer. They call me Mort.

YSABELL
I shall call you Boy.

MORT
Excuse me, but who are you?

YSABELL
I'm Ysabell. His daughter.

MORT
His daughter? Death's daughter?

YSABELL
Adopted, of course. Why did he bring you here?

MORT
He hired me at the Hiring Fair. I'm his apprentice.

(YSABELL turns to the door and shouts)

YSABELL
Albert! Another one for breakfast! *(turns back to MORT)* Well, I must say, that with the whole Disc to choose from, he might have done better than you. I suppose you'll have to do.

(She sweeps out. There is a brief pause)

MORT
Have to do what?

(ALBERT puts his head round the door. He carries a grease-blackened frying pan, with two fried eggs in it)

ALBERT
One egg or two?

MORT *(breaking out of his reverie)*
What? Sorry, what did you say?

ALBERT
I said, one egg or two.

MORT
  Oh, er, one please.

ALBERT
  Right you are, young sir.

(He starts to leave)

MORT
  Er, excuse me. Where am I exactly?

ALBERT
  Don't you know? This is the House of Death, lad. He
  brought you here last night on his mighty white steed,
  Binky.

MORT
  BINKY?! I would have thought Death's horse would be
  called Ebony or Sabre.

ALBERT
  Or Fang. Nope, it's just one of the Master's little fancies.
  He used to have a proper, skeletal horse, but he had to
  keep stopping to wire bits back on. And the fiery steed
  used to keep burning the stable down. So now it's a real
  horse. Binky.

(DEATH enters. He carries a large book)

DEATH
AH, ALBERT, GOOD MORNING. TWO EGGS
FOR ME, PLEASE.

(Albert exits. Death sits at his desk, then looks up)

WHO ARE YOU, BOY?

MORT
Mort, sir. Your apprentice. Don't you remember?

DEATH
OH YES. MORT. WELL, BOY, DO YOU SIN-
CERELY WISH TO LEARN THE UTTERMOST
SECRETS OF TIME AND SPACE?

MORT
Yes, sir. I think so, sir.

DEATH
GOOD. THE STABLES ARE ROUND THE
BACK. THE SHOVEL HANGS JUST INSIDE THE
DOOR. *(MORT doesn't move)* IS IT BY ANY
CHANCE POSSIBLE THAT YOU DON'T
UNDERSTAND ME?

MORT
Not fully, sir.

DEATH
DUNG, BOY. DUNG. ALBERT HAS A COMPOST
HEAP IN THE GARDEN. I IMAGINE THERE'S A
WHEELBARROW SOMEWHERE. GET ON WITH
IT.

(DEATH sits at the desk and pores over the book)

MORT
Yes, sir. I see, sir. *(pause)* Sir?

DEATH
YES.

MORT
Sir, I don't see what this has to do with the secrets of time
and space.

DEATH
THAT, IS BECAUSE YOU ARE HERE TO LEARN.

(Lights black out as MORT exits. Ysabell enters into a follow-spot)

YSABELL
I can't imagine why father bothered to bring that boy
here. How can you learn to be Death? Anyway, Mort
soon finds out that not only is Death's horse a real, flesh
and blood animal, but he's also very well fed. Some jobs
offer you increments . . . this one offers, well, quite the
reverse, really. And serve him right!

(Lights black out)

SCENE 3 – DEATH'S STUDY

(Later that day. DEATH is on stage, studying an atlas. MORT enters)

DEATH
YOU HAVEN'T HEARD OF THE BAY OF MANTE, HAVE YOU?

MORT
No, sir.

DEATH
FAMOUS SHIP-WRECK THERE.

MORT
Was there?

DEATH
THERE WILL BE, IF I CAN FIND THE DAMN PLACE.

MORT
You're going to sink the ship?

DEATH
CERTAINLY NOT! THERE WILL BE A COMBI-
NATION OF BAD SEAMANSHIP, SHALLOW
WATER AND A CONTRARY WIND.

MORT
That's horrible. Will there be many drowned?

DEATH
THAT'S UP TO FATE. THERE'S NOTHING I
CAN DO ABOUT IT. *(pause)* WHAT IS THAT
SMELL?

MORT
Me.

DEATH
AH. THE STABLES. AND WHY DO YOU THINK
I DIRECTED YOU TO THE STABLES? THINK
CAREFULLY NOW.

MORT
Well, at first I wondered if it was to co-ordinate my hand
and eye, or to teach me the habit of obedience, or to
bring home to me the importance of trivial tasks, or to
make me realise that even great men must start at the
bottom.

DEATH
YES?

MORT
Well, I think it was because you were up to your knees in horse-shit, to tell the truth.

DEATH
ABSOLUTELY CORRECT. CLARITY OF THOUGHT. REALISTIC APPROACH. VERY IMPORTANT IN A JOB LIKE OURS. IF YOU LIKE YOU CAN COME OUT ON THE ROUND WITH ME THIS EVENING. *(He rings a bell on his desk)* HAVE YOU MET MY DAUGHTER?

MORT
Er, yes, sir.

DEATH
SHE IS A VERY PLEASANT GIRL, BUT I THINK SHE QUITE LIKES HAVING SOMEONE OF HER OWN AGE TO TALK TO.

MORT
Sir?

DEATH
AND OF COURSE, ONE DAY ALL THIS WILL BELONG TO HER.

(ALBERT enters)

AH, ALBERT, WHEN YOU GO AND GET THE HORSE READY, THE BOY CAN HELP YOU.

MORT
  Mort.

(DEATH exits)

  He said I could go out with him tonight.

ALBERT
  You're a lucky boy, then.

MORT
  Did he really make all this?

ALBERT
  Yes.

MORT
  Why?

ALBERT
  I suppose he wanted somewhere where he could feel at home.

MORT
  Are you dead, Albert?

ALBERT
  Me? Do I look dead?

MORT
  Sorry.

ALBERT
Right. It's best not to ask these questions, it upsets
people. Do you know what happens to boys who ask too
many questions?

MORT
No. What?

ALBERT
Damned if I know. Looking forward to it, are you?

MORT
I think so. I've never seen Death actually at work.

ALBERT
Not many have. Not twice at any rate.

(They start to exit as the lights black out)

SCENE 4 – THE CASTLE OF STO LAT

(Evening. There are courtiers on stage and servants with trays of drinks. Also on stage are KELI, the KING and the DUKE OF STO HELIT)

KING
    . . . and then the first witch said, 'I know, the black one's bigger than the white one.'

(The GUESTS all laugh, particularly STO HELIT)

STO HELIT
    Very funny, sire. Lords and ladies, a toast to our sovereign; to Olerve the Bastard. Congratulations on your silver jubilee, sire. Here's to the next twenty-five years.

(As the GUESTS toast the KING, MORT and DEATH enter, unseen. During the scene, the GUESTS mingle around, managing to avoid MORT and DEATH without apparently being aware of their presence)

MORT
    Where are we?

DEATH
    THE CASTLE OF STO LAT. ONE RATHER IMPORTANT ASSASSINATION. A KING.

MORT

I'd quite like to see a real king. They wear their crowns
all the time, my granny says. Even when they go to the
lavatory.

DEATH

THERE'S NO TECHNICAL REASON WHY NOT.
IN MY EXPERIENCE, HOWEVER, IT IS GENER-
ALLY NOT THE CASE. WE'VE GOT A FEW
MINUTES, LET'S MINGLE.

(He takes the last drink from a passing tray. The servant moves
on, without pausing, to offer the now empty tray to one of the
guests. Confused looks)

MORT

I've watched people. They look at you but they don't see
you. Do you do something to their minds?

DEATH

THEY DO IT THEMSELVES. THEY WON'T
ALLOW THEMSELVES TO SEE ME. UNTIL IT'S
TIME, OF COURSE. WIZARDS CAN SEE ME.
AND CATS. BUT NOT ORDINARY HUMANS.
STRANGE BUT TRUE.

MORT

They can't see me either! But I'm real!

DEATH

IF THEY DON'T WANT TO SEE ME, THEY CER-
TAINLY DON'T WANT TO SEE YOU. THESE

ARE ARISTOCRATS, BOY. THEY'RE GOOD AT NOT SEEING THINGS. WHY IS THERE A CHERRY ON A STICK IN THIS DRINK?

MORT
Mort.

DEATH
IT'S NOT AS IF IT DOES ANYTHING FOR THE FLAVOUR. WHY DOES ANYONE TAKE A PERFECTLY GOOD DRINK AND THEN PUT IN A CHERRY ON A POLE?

MORT
Pardon?

DEATH
THAT'S MORTALS FOR YOU. THEY'VE ONLY GOT A FEW YEARS IN THIS WORLD AND THEY SPEND THEM ALL IN MAKING THINGS COMPLICATED FOR THEMSELVES. FASCINATING. HAVE A DRINK.

MORT
Which one's the king?

DEATH
HE'S THE ONE OVER THERE, GETTING ALL THE LAUGHS.

(The KING has just cracked a joke. The COURTIERS laugh, including STO HELIT)

MORT
   He doesn't look like a bad king. Why would anyone want
   to kill him?

DEATH
   SEE THE MAN NEXT TO HIM, WITH THE EVIL
   GRIN?

MORT
   Yes?

DEATH
   HIS COUSIN, THE DUKE OF STO HELIT. NOT
   THE NICEST OF PEOPLE. A HANDY MAN
   WITH A BOTTLE OF POISON. FIFTH IN LINE
   TO THE THRONE LAST YEAR. NOW SECOND
   IN LINE. BIT OF A SOCIAL CLIMBER, YOU
   MIGHT SAY. *(examines an hour-glass at his waist)*
   AND DUE TO LIVE ANOTHER THIRTY,
   THIRTY-FIVE YEARS. *(sighs)*

MORT
   And he goes around killing people? There's no justice.

DEATH *(sighing)*
   NO. THERE'S ONLY ME. *(starts to draw his sword)*

MORT
   I thought you used a scythe.

DEATH
KINGS GET THE SWORD. IT'S A ROYAL
WOSSNAME, PREROGATIVE. PAY CARE-
FUL ATTENTION, YOU MAY BE ASKED
QUESTIONS AFTERWARDS.

MORT
It's not fair. Can't you stop it?

DEATH
FAIR? YOU CAN'T TAKE SIDES. GOOD GRIEF.
WHEN IT'S TIME, IT'S TIME. THAT'S ALL
THERE IS TO IT, BOY.

MORT
Mort.

(Suddenly MORT catches sight of KELI. For a second, she
thinks she sees him, too, and starts to cross the room to him.
Then, shaking her head, she turns and rejoins the group.
DEATH nudges MORT)

DEATH
IT'S TIME. FOLLOW ME.

(He starts to cross the stage to the KING. KELI turns again
and looks in MORT's direction)

MORT (to the KING)
Look out! You're in great danger!

(The STROBE starts as DEATH raises his sword. The action is in slow-motion. The KING reacts as he is 'hit in the back by a crossbow bolt'. DEATH swings the sword, the STROBE stops and a blue follow-spot comes up on the KING (now dead). As the King dies, he sheds his overgown, which then 'becomes' his corpse – a bit of gimcrack symbolism for them as likes it!)

DEATH *(to MORT)*
    A GOOD CLEAN JOB.

KING *(to DEATH)*
    Who the hell are you? What are you doing here? Guards!
    I demand . . . Oh. I see. I didn't expect to see you so soon.

DEATH
    FEW DO, YOUR MAJESTY.

(The KING looks over his shoulder at the bolt in his back)

KING
    Clean job. Crossbow was it? *(DEATH nods)* Who did it?

DEATH
    A HIRED ASSASSIN FROM ANKH-MORPORK.

KING
    Clever. I congratulate Sto Helit. And here's me filling
    myself with antidotes. No antidote to cold steel, eh?

DEATH
    INDEED NOT, SIRE.

KING

The old rope ladder and fast horse by the drawbridge, eh?

DEATH

YES, SIRE. IF IT'S ANY CONSOLATION, THE HORSE NEEDS TO BE FAST.

KING

Eh?

DEATH

I HAVE AN APPOINTMENT WITH ITS RIDER TOMORROW IN ANKH. YOU SEE, HE ALLOWED THE DUKE TO PROVIDE HIM WITH A PACKED LUNCH.

(KELI is kneeling by the KING's body, sobbing. STO HELIT puts a comforting arm around KELI)

MORT

I can't make you hear me. Don't trust him.

(KELI peers vaguely at MORT)

DEATH

COME ALONG NOW, BOY. NO LALLYGAG-GING.

MORT

Mort.

DEATH
WHAT?

MORT
My name is Mort. Or Mortimer. What's happened to the King?

DEATH
ONLY HE KNOWS.

MORT
My granny says that dying is like falling asleep.

DEATH
I WOULDN'T KNOW. I HAVE DONE NEITHER. YOU TRIED TO WARN HIM.

MORT
Yes, sir. Sorry.

DEATH
YOU CANNOT INTERFERE WITH FATE. WHO ARE YOU TO SAY WHO SHOULD LIVE AND WHO SHOULD DIE? ONLY THE GODS ARE ALLOWED TO DO THAT. TO TINKER WITH THE FATE OF EVEN ONE INDIVIDUAL COULD DESTROY THE WHOLE WORLD. DO YOU UNDERSTAND?

MORT
Are you going to send me home?

DEATH
BECAUSE YOU SHOWED COMPASSION? NO. I
MIGHT HAVE DONE IF YOU HAD SHOWN
PLEASURE. BUT YOU MUST LEARN THE
COMPASSION PROPER TO YOUR TRADE.

MORT
What's that?

DEATH
A SHARP EDGE.

*(Tableau of STO HELIT comforting KELI. As DEATH
and MORT leave the stage, the lights black out to be replaced
by a follow-spot on ALBERT, who has entered, carrying a
frying pan and scourer)*

ALBERT
Well, that was Mort's first task as Death's apprentice. As
the days passed, he did many more visits with the Master
– not just kings and important battles – most of the personal visits were to quite ordinary people. Mort still
mucked out the stables, and helped me in the kitchen . . .
and spent time in Death's library reading the life histories. They write themselves you know. Dead people's
books are full up. Unborn people's books are all blank
pages. Everyone else's are scribbling away to themselves,
writing down everything folk do. Anyway, after a few
weeks, Mort decided to ask Death for a favour.

(Light out on ALBERT as the light goes up for the next scene)

SCENE 5 – DEATH'S LIBRARY

(Some time later. DEATH is on stage, with MORT)

DEATH
A WHAT?

MORT
An afternoon off.

DEATH
BUT WHY? IT CAN'T BE TO ATTEND YOUR
GRANDMOTHER'S FUNERAL. I WOULD
KNOW.

MORT
I just want to, you know, get out and meet people.

DEATH
BUT YOU MEET PEOPLE EVERY DAY.

MORT
Yes, but not for very long. I mean, it'd be nice to meet
someone with a life expectancy of more than a few minutes. Sir.

DEATH
ALL RIGHT. ANKH-MORPORK HAS ABOUT AS

MANY PEOPLE AS EVEN YOU COULD WISH.
BUT IT SEEMS TO ME YOU HAVE EVERY-
THING YOU NEED RIGHT HERE. YOU HAVE
GOOD FOOD AND A WARM BED AND PEOPLE
OF YOUR OWN AGE.

MORT
Pardon, sir?

DEATH
MY DAUGHTER. YOU HAVE MET HER I
BELIEVE.

MORT
Oh. Yes, sir.

DEATH
SHE HAS A WARM PERSONALITY WHEN YOU
GET TO KNOW HER. NEVERTHELESS, YOU
WISH AN AFTERNOON OFF?

MORT
Yes, sir. If you please, sir.

DEATH
VERY WELL. YOU MAY HAVE UNTIL SUNSET.
(He starts to look through a ledger. MORT does not move)
YOU'RE STILL HERE. AND IN YOUR OWN
TIME, TOO.

MORT
Um, will people be able to see me, sir?

DEATH

I IMAGINE SO. IS THERE ANYTHING ELSE I
MIGHT BE ABLE TO ASSIST YOU WITH
BEFORE YOU LEAVE FOR THIS DEBAUCH?

MORT

Just one thing, sir. How do I get to the mortal world?

DEATH

JUST WALK THERE. *(small pause)* BOY. *(He throws
a bag of coins to MORT)*

(MORT exits. ALBERT enters with a ledger)

ALBERT

Just three tonight, sir. Goodie Hamstring, the Abbott
Lobsang again and the Princess Keli.

DEATH

I WAS THINKING OF SENDING THE LAD OUT
ON HIS OWN.

ALBERT

Well, Goodie wouldn't be any trouble, and the Abbott is
what you'd call experienced. Shame about the Princess.
Only twenty-two. Could be tricky.

DEATH

YES, IT IS A PITY. ONE SO YOUNG. ANKH-
MORPORK. ANKH-MORPORK. AS FULL OF
LIFE AS AN OLD CHEESE ON A HOT DAY;
AS LOUD AS A CURSE IN A CATHEDRAL; AS

33

COLOURFUL AS A BRUISE AND AS FULL OF
INDUSTRY, BUSTLE AND SHEER BUSYNESS
AS . . . AS . . .

ALBERT
. . . as a dead dog on a termite mound. Are you all right,
Master?

DEATH
WHAT? I HAVE NEVER FELT BETTER. AN
AFTERNOON OFF, HE SAID. AN AFTERNOON
OFF. WHAT . . . FUN.

(Black out)

SCENE 6 – OUTSIDE CUTWELL'S EMPORIUM/
INSIDE CUTWELL'S EMPORIUM

(The DOORKNOCKER is on stage. TOWNCRIER enters. He speaks throughout in the same shouting tone he uses for his town crier announcements)

TOWNCRIER
Nine o'clock and all's well! Nine o'clock . . . !

(CUTWELL's head appears)

Hello, Cutwell!

CUTWELL
What's new?

TOWNCRIER
Not much! Lot of tradesmen have seen a gangly youth! who keeps trying to walk through walls! I just seen him meself, in the Broken Drum in Filigree Street! He was looking a bit bruised! and asking the landlord to point him in the direction of the nearest wizard!

CUTWELL
Oh hell.

TOWNCRIER
Nine o'clock and all's well!

(He exits. A pause. MORT enters. He crosses to the door of CUTWELL's emporium. There is a large card on the door, which he reads)

MORT
'Igneous Cutwell, DM (Unseen University), Marster of the Infinit, Iluminartus, Wyzard to Princes, Gardian of the Sacred Portalls, If Out leave Maile with Mrs Nugent next door.'

(He knocks at the door)

DOORKNOCKER
Oh, hello. He won't be a minute. He'll juft be tidying away hif old focks and hiding the waffing up.

(CUTWELL appears at a window)

CUTWELL
Beneficent constellations shine on the hour of our meeting!

MORT
Which ones?

CUTWELL
Pardon?

MORT
    Which constellations would these be?

CUTWELL *(uncertainly)*
    Beneficent ones. Why do you trouble Igneous Cutwell,
    Holder of the Eight Keys, Traveller in the Dungeon
    Dimensions, Supreme Mage of . . .

MORT
    Excuse me, are you really?

CUTWELL
    Really what?

MORT
    Master of the Thingy, Lord High Wossname of the
    Sacred Dungeons?

CUTWELL
    Figuratively.

MORT
    What does that mean?

CUTWELL
    Well, it means no.

MORT
    But you said . . .

CUTWELL
    That was advertising. It's a kind of magic I've been

working on. What was it you were wanting, anyway? A love philtre, yes? Something to encourage the young ladies? *(taps side of nose with finger)*

MORT
Is it possible to walk through walls?

CUTWELL
Using magic?

MORT
Um, I don't think so.

CUTWELL
Then choose very thin walls, or doors, even.

(MORT jangles his purse of coins in front of CUTWELL. CUTWELL makes a whinnying noise in his throat)

MORT *(slowly and deliberately)*
I've walked through walls.

CUTWELL
Of course you have, of course you have.

MORT
Only before I did it I didn't know I could, and when I was doing it I didn't know I was, and now I've done it I can't remember how it was done, and I want to do it again. I've been trying for all the afternoon, but I only managed it once when I didn't mean to. Can you help?

38

CUTWELL
Why?

MORT
Because if I could walk through walls, I could do anything.

CUTWELL
Very deep. And the name of the young lady on the other
side of this wall?

MORT
She's . . . I don't know her name. Even if there is a girl.
And I'm not saying there is.

CUTWELL
Right. Fine. How to walk through walls. I'll do some
research. It might be expensive, though.

(MORT takes out one coin and gives it to CUTWELL)

MORT
A down payment.

CUTWELL
What sort of coin's this? I've never seen one like it. It's
gold, all right, but how did you come by it?

MORT
You wouldn't believe me. I need to get to Sto Lat. *(He
looks around him)* What time's sunset around here?

CUTWELL
We normally manage to fit it in between night and day.
About now, in fact.

MORT
Oh, ye gods, I'm late! And I don't know how to get back!
(to CUTWELL) Look into it for me, please. I'll call
again!

*(CUTWELL goes. MORT crosses the stage to exit. As he
reaches the exit, DEATH suddenly appears before him. He is
carrying a bag of chips) [NOTE – we made the chips out of
yellow foam, and had them in a cone made of a copy of the
'Ankh-Morpork Gazette', a newspaper we'd spoofed up for
Death to read in a later scene]*

DEATH
AH, BOY. HAVE A CHIP. *(MORT shakes his head)* I
THOUGHT YOU'D LIKE TO DO THE ROUND
ON YOUR OWN TONIGHT.

MORT
By myself?

DEATH
CERTAINLY. I HAVE EVERY FAITH IN YOU.

MORT
Gosh!

DEATH
THINK YOU CAN DO IT?

MORT
Well, sir. Yes, I think.

DEATH
THAT'S THE SPIRIT. I'VE LEFT BINKY AT
THE HORSE TROUGH ROUND THE CORNER.
TAKE HIM STRAIGHT HOME WHEN YOU'VE
FINISHED.

MORT
You're staying here, sir?

DEATH
I THOUGHT I MIGHT STROLL AROUND A
BIT. I DON'T SEEM TO FEEL QUITE RIGHT.
I COULD DO WITH A LITTLE TIME OFF.

(He hands MORT three hourglasses and a cloak)

ALL STRAIGHTFORWARD. ENJOY YOURSELF.
ER, HAVE . . . FUN.

(DEATH exits. MORT calls after him)

MORT
Um. Thank you. Does this mean I'm in charge?

*(A short pause. MORT puts on the cloak, swirls it and laughs,
as the lights black out. Spotlight up on CUTWELL. He speaks
as Mort and Binky are seen flying off to Goodie Hamstring's)*

CUTWELL

Mort's in charge, eh? First call was at Goodie Hamstring's cottage. Goodie is a witch. Her cottage stands in a clearing in the middle of a forest. The trees hadn't been cut down round her cottage, they'd just been discouraged from growing.

(Lights swap to next scene)

SCENE 7 – GOODIE HAMSTRING'S KITCHEN

(Just a chair on stage, with GOODIE HAMSTRING, a 'bloody ole witch', sat on it, writing. She is wearing a large woollen cloak and has white hair. She is very bowed with age. [NOTE – we had our Goodie Hamstring in her floaty, post-death outfit under an all-covering long black hooded robe and a character 'witch' nose and white wig] MORT enters silently, carrying the scythe)

HAMSTRING
  Be with you in a moment. I haven't put in the bit about being of sound mind yet. A lot of foolishness anyway, no-one sound in mind and body would be dead. Would you like a drink?

MORT
  Pardon? I mean PARDON?

HAMSTRING
  There's a bottle of raspberry port on the dresser. You may as well finish it if you want.

(MORT takes out an hourglass and looks at it crossly)

HAMSTRING
  There's still a few minutes left.

MORT
How, I mean, HOW DO YOU KNOW? Er, I haven't, that is I HAVEN'T GOT ALL DAY YOU KNOW.

HAMSTRING
You have, I haven't, and there's no need to shout. Will I need my shawl, do you think? I imagine it's quite warm where I'm going. *(She peers at MORT)* You're rather younger than I imagined. You know, I don't think you're who I was expecting at all.

MORT
Who were you expecting, precisely?

HAMSTRING
Death.

MORT
He sent me. I work for him. No-one else would have me. No, no, no, this is all wrong! This is my first real job and it's all going wrong!

(MORT starts to wail. He drops the scythe)

HAMSTRING
I see. What is your name, young man?

MORT *(sniffing)*
Mort. Short for Mortimer.

HAMSTRING
Well, Mort, I expect you've got an hour-glass some-where about your person?

(MORT nods and draws out the glass. HAMSTRING looks at it)

Still about a minute left, but we should get on with it, though.

MORT
But you don't understand! I'll mess it all up! I've never done this before!

HAMSTRING
Neither have I. We can learn together. Now pick up the scythe and try to act your own age, there's a good boy.

MORT *(picking up the scythe)*
I can't believe all this. I mean you sound as though you want to die.

HAMSTRING
There's some things I shall miss. But it gets thin – life, I mean. You can't trust your own body any more, and it's time to move on. Did you know magical folk can see him?

MORT
He doesn't like wizards and witches much.

HAMSTRING
Nobody likes a smartass. We give him trouble, you see.

Priests don't, so he likes priests. They're always telling folk how much better it's going to be when they're dead. We tell them it could be pretty good right here if they'd only put their minds to it.

MORT
You're wrong, he's not like that. He doesn't care if people are good or bad so long as they're punctual. And kind to cats.

HAMSTRING
Maybe. It's time.

(MORT swings the scythe. Strobe effect. The actress turns her back on the audience; she removes the nose and wig in one movement and drops them, with the black robe, on the floor. She turns to face MORT. She looks stunning)

Well done. I thought you'd missed it, for a minute there.

What do you think, Mort?

(MORT makes a small noise in his throat)

I didn't hear you.

MORT
V–v–very nice. Is that who you were?

HAMSTRING
It's who I've always been.

MORT

Oh. I–I'm supposed to take you away.

HAMSTRING

I know. But I'm going to stay.

MORT

You can't do that! I mean . . . you see, if you stay you sort of spread out and get thinner, until . . .

HAMSTRING

I shall enjoy it. *(She kisses her finger and puts it to MORT's forehead)* Have a care, Mort. You may want to hold on to your job, but will you ever be able to let go?

(She exits. MORT suddenly realises the time, looks at the next hour glass and dashes off)

SCENE 8 – MONASTERY OF THE HOLY LISTENERS

(The ABBOTT is on stage, kneeling in prayer. His 'Ommm!' is heard in the dark before the lights come up. MORT charges on, out of breath)

ABBOTT
  You're late.

(MORT swings the scythe. Strobe effect) [We had our ABBOTT in CofE Bishop's vestments, so that, on death, he cast off his embroidered cope]

  Not a moment too soon. You had me worried for a moment there.

MORT *(making for the door)*
  OK? Only I've got to rush.

ABBOTT
  Don't rush off. I always look forward to these little talks. What's happened to the usual fellow?

MORT
  Usual fellow?

ABBOTT

Tall chap. Black cloak. Doesn't get enough to eat, by the look of him.

MORT

Usual fellow? You mean Death?

ABBOTT

That's him.

MORT

Die a lot, do you?

ABBOTT

A fair bit. A fair bit. Of course, once you get the hang of it, it's only a matter of practice.

MORT

It is?

ABBOTT

We must be off.

MORT

That's what I've been trying to say.

ABBOTT

So if you could just drop me off down in the valley.

MORT

Now look . . .

ABBOTT
The other one had a horse called Binky, I remember. Did you buy the franchise off him?

MORT
The franchise?

ABBOTT
Or whatever. Forgive me. I don't really know how these things are organised, lad.

MORT
Mort. And I think you're supposed to come back with me, sir.

ABBOTT
I wish I could. Perhaps one day. Now, if you could give me a lift as far as the nearest village, I imagine I'm being conceived about now.

MORT
Conceived? But you've just died!

ABBOTT
Yes, but you see, I have what you might call a season ticket.

MORT
Oh. I've read about this. Reincarnation, yes?

ABBOTT
That's the word. Fifty-three times so far. Or fifty-four.

MORT

It must be interesting.

ABBOTT

No it mustn't. You think it must be because you believe I can remember all my lives, but of course I can't. Not while I'm alive, anyway.

MORT

I hadn't thought of that.

ABBOTT

Imagine toilet training fifty times. If I had my time again I wouldn't reincarnate. And just when I'm getting the hang of things, the lads come down from the temple looking for a boy conceived at the hour the old abbott died. Talk about unimaginative.

MORT

I hope the next lifetime improves.

ABBOTT

One can always hope. I get a nine-month break anyway. The scenery isn't much, but at least it's in the warm.

MORT

Come on, then, I've got to rush.

ABBOTT *(as they exit)*

I expect I'll see you again, sometime.

(And the lights black out)

SCENE 9 – PRINCESS KELI'S ROOM IN STO HELIT CASTLE

(It is dark. The ASSASSIN lurks on stage, wielding a sword. KELI enters, in a peignoir, carrying a lighted candle)

KELI
Who's there? I can hear you. Answer me, or I shall summon the guard.

ASSASSIN
Highness, I am the guard. Don't bother to call out, nobody will hear you. Please accept my apologies, Highness, I am acting under orders.

KELI
My uncle, the Duke of Sto Helit, I imagine.

ASSASSIN
Yes, Highness. It won't hurt, Highness, I have sharpened the blade with surgical precision.

(MORT bursts in, scythe at the ready. The ASSASSIN turns, but MORT strikes him with the scythe)

MORT
If you scream, I'll regret it. Please? I'm in enough trouble as it is.

KELI

Who are you?

MORT

I don't know if I'm allowed to tell you. You are still alive, aren't you?

KELI

Can't you tell?

MORT

It's not easy . . . I may have done you some terrible harm.

KELI

Haven't you just saved my life?

MORT

I don't know what I've saved actually.

KELI

Haven't I seen you somewhere before?

MORT

Er, possibly.

KELI

Well, first you'd better tell me why I shouldn't send for the guards anyway. Even being in my rooms can get you tortured to death.

MORT

All right. I am Death's apprentice. I was supposed to

come here tonight for your assassination. See? *(He holds up the hourglass)* And now I've stopped the assassination and I don't know what will happen now.

KELI
  You're Death's apprentice? You?

MORT
  Yes. Look out into the corridor.

(KELI does so. Binky whinnies)

KELI
  It's a horse. How did you get a horse up here?

(MORT shrugs, modestly)

  All right, you're Death's apprentice. I still don't understand this. Does this mean I'm dead, or not?

MORT
  It means you ought to be dead, according to fate or whatever. I haven't really studied the theory.

KELI
  And you should have killed me?

MORT
  No! The assassin should have killed you.

KELI
  Why didn't you let him?

MORT

Did you want to die?

KELI

Of course I didn't. But it looks as though what people
want doesn't come into it, does it? I'm trying to be sen-
sible about this.

MORT *(sighing)*

I think I'd better be going. Watch out for the Duke. He's
behind this.

KELI

Shall I see you again? There's lots of . . .

MORT

That might not be a good idea. If you think about it.

KELI

Oh. Right.

*(A MAID enters as MORT exits, but she successfully avoids
him whilst seeming to not notice him)*

MAID

Are you all right, ma'am?

KELI

What?

MAID *(She is living the 'real' reality, where KELI has just been killed. She can't work out in her mind why she needed to see if KELI was all right)*

I just wondered if . . . everything was all right?

KELI
No. Everything's all wrong. There's a dead assassin on my floor. Could you please have something done about it?

(The MAID opens her mouth to speak)

And – I don't want you to say 'Dead, Ma'am?' or 'Assassin, Ma'am?' or scream or anything. I just want you to get something done about it. Quietly. I think I've got a headache. So just nod.

(The MAID just nods, bobs uncertainly and backs away as the lights black out)

SCENE 10 – DEATH'S LIBRARY

(MORT is on stage, reading through a book, by candlelight)

MORT
' . . . the princess's assassination at the age of twenty-two
was followed by the union of Sto Lat with Sto Helit and,
indirectly, the collapse of the city states of the central
plain and the rise of . . . mumble . . . mumble . . . under
the Duke of Sto Helit a new peace descended on the
land.' *(He groans)* I must tell someone.

*(MORT closes the book with a bang. There is a gasp and a
scuffling noise off-stage)*

Who's there? Albert?

*(MORT exits and re-enters, carrying two open volumes. On
the top one is a lacy hanky. MORT looks at it quizzically.
There is another noise off and ALBERT enters)*

ALBERT
Yes, what did you want?

MORT
Sorry?

ALBERT
You called out my name.

MORT
Oh. Yes. Er . . .

ALBERT
What you got there?

MORT *(looking at the book)*
Oh. It's, er . . . 'Princess Keli'.

ALBERT
Hmm. Master wants to see you. Said you wasn't to rush, though. He said he hadn't had an evening off in a thousand years. He was humming. I don't like it. I've never seen him like this.

(MORT has been building up his courage to speak to ALBERT)

MORT
Erm. Albert, have you been here long?

ALBERT
Maybe. It's hard to keep track of outside time, boy. I bin here since just after the old king died.

MORT
Which king was that?

ALBERT
  Artorollo, I think he was called. Little fat man. Squeaky
  voice.

MORT
  Where was this?

ALBERT
  In Ankh-Morpork, of course.

MORT
  What? They don't have kings in Ankh-Morpork, everyone knows that! The city's ruled by the Patrician. He's a
  sort of dictator. My mum says it's a democracy – one
  man, one vote. The Patrician's the man; he's got the
  vote.

ALBERT
  This was a bit back, I said. And they was kings in those
  days, real kings, not like the sort you get now. They was
  monarchs. I mean, they was wise and fair, well, fairly
  wise. And they wouldn't think twice about having your
  head cut off soon as look at you. And the queens were tall
  and pale and wore them balaclava things on their heads.

MORT
  Wimples?

ALBERT
  Yeah, them, and the princesses were beautiful as the day
  is long and so noble they, they could pee through a dozen
  mattresses . . .

MORT
What?

ALBERT
Something like that, anyway. And there was balls and
tournaments and executions. Great days.

MORT
Have you any other names, Albert?

ALBERT
Oh I know. Get Albert's name and come and look him
up in Library, eh? Prying and poking. I know you, skulk-
ing in at all hours reading the lives of young wimmen.

MORT
Wha . . .

ALBERT
You might at least put them back where you find 'em . . .
not leave piles of them for old Albert to put back. It's not
right, ogling the poor things. You'll go blind.

(and ALBERT exits, grumbling)

MORT
But I only . . .

(He looks down at the lace hanky and sighs)

So much for Albert. I'll have to tell Death himself . . .

(Lights black out)

SCENE 11 – SPOTLIGHT ON ALBERT, OPENING TO EXTERIOR, CUTWELL'S

ALBERT

Oh dear. The course of true love, and so on, eh? And Princess Keli is also finding life difficult. Bluntly, the universe knew she was dead, so it was rather surprised to find that she hadn't stopped walking and breathing yet. Wherever she went, people ignored her.

The Chamberlain found that he had ordered the flags to be flown at half mast, but he couldn't explain why. Through all this, the Princess Keli moved like a solid and increasingly more irritated ghost.

(KELI storms across the stage and bangs on CUTWELL's door. ALBERT exits. A face appears at the window (CUTWELL))

KELI

I demand to see the wizard. Pray admit me this instant.

CUTWELL

He's rather busy at present. Did you want a love potion? Provides your wild oats while guaranteeing a crop failure, if you know what I mean.

KELI

No. I do not. Look, I have travelled all the way from Sto Lat. I demand—

CUTWELL

Sorry. We're closed.

(and he is gone. KELI knocks again. Then realisation!)

KELI

Hold on . . . he saw me! He heard me!

(She knocks again)

DOORKNOCKER

It won't work. He'f very ftubborn.

KELI

I am Princess Keli, heir to the throne of Sto Lat. And I don't talk to door furniture.

DOORKNOCKER

Fwell, I'm just a doorknocker and I can talk to fwhoever I please. And I can tell you that the fmaster iff having a trying day and duff not fwant to be difturbed. But you could try to use the magic word. Coming from an attractiff woman it works nine times out of eight.

KELI

Magic word? What is the magic word?

DOORKNOCKER
Haff you been taught nothing, miff?

KELI
I have been *educated* by some of the finest scholars on the Disc.

DOORKNOCKER
Iff they didn't teach you the magic word, they couldn't haff been all that fine.

(KELI bangs loudly on the door. The head appears again)

CUTWELL
I said we're closed.

KELI
Please help me! Please!

DOORKNOCKER
See? Sooner or later, everyone remembers the magic word!

(As KELI enters, the lights crossfade to CUTWELL's room)

CUTWELL
Now, how can I help you? Sorry it's a bit untidy. It's Mrs Nugent's day off.

KELI

I have a problem, Mr Cutwell, and I have travelled over twenty miles to consult you.

CUTWELL

Right. Hang on. *(He picks up his hat, removes from it a slice of pizza, puts on his hat)* Right. Fire away.

KELI

What's so important about the hat?

CUTWELL

Oh, it's very essential. You've got to have the proper hat for wizarding. We wizards know about this kind of thing.

KELI

If you say so. Look, can you see me?

CUTWELL *(peering at her)*

Yes. I would say that I can definitely see you.

KELI

Then would you be surprised to learn that no-one else in this city can? I talk to them and they keep looking away. I'm a princess – I'm not used to that sort of treatment. Why can't anyone see me?

CUTWELL

Except me?

KELI

And your doorknocker!

CUTWELL
Do you feel invisible?

KELI
No. Just angry. I want you to tell my fortune.

CUTWELL
It's illegal, you see. The old king expressly forbade fortune-telling in Sto Lat. He didn't like wizards much.

KELI
I can pay. A lot.

CUTWELL
Mrs Nugent was telling me this new girl is likely to be worse. A right haughty one, she said. Not the sort to look kindly on practitioners of the subtle arts, I fear.

(KELI smiles in a threatening way, but CUTWELL misses it)

KELI
I understand she's got a foul temper on her. I wouldn't be surprised if she didn't turn you out of the city anyway.

CUTWELL
Oh dear. Do you think so?

KELI

Look, you don't have to tell my future. Just my present. Even she couldn't object to that. I'll have a word with her, if you like.

CUTWELL

You know her?

KELI

Yes. But sometimes, I think, not well.

CUTWELL *(picking up the Caroc deck)*

Well . . . these are the Caroc cards. Distilled wisdom of the Ancients and all that. Pick a card. Any card.

KELI

It's Death.

CUTWELL

Ah. Well. Of course, the Death card doesn't actually mean death in all circumstances.

KELI

You mean it doesn't mean death in those circumstances where the subject is getting over-excited and you're too embarrassed to tell the truth, hmm?

CUTWELL

Look, take another card.

KELI

This one's Death as well.

CUTWELL
Did you put the other one back?

KELI
No. Shall I take another card?

CUTWELL
May as well.

KELI
Well, there's a coincidence.

CUTWELL
Death number three?

KELI
Right. Is this a special pack for conjuring tricks?

(CUTWELL examines the pack. It is quite normal. He pulls out a card; it is the Fool)

CUTWELL
Oh dear. I think this is going to be serious. May I see the palm of your hand, please?

(He examines it for a long while, using a magnifying glass and a pair of protractors and ruler)

You're dead. It could be fatal.

KELI
How much more fatal than being dead?

CUTWELL

I didn't mean for you.

KELI

Oh.

CUTWELL

Something very fundamental seems to have gone wrong, you see. You're dead in every sense but the, er, actual. I mean, the cards think you're dead, your lifeline thinks you're dead. Everyone thinks you're dead.

KELI

I don't.

CUTWELL

I'm afraid your opinion doesn't count.

KELI

But people can still hear and see me! If I hit them hard enough!

CUTWELL

Now look, I'm a graduate of Unseen University – that's the university for wizards in Ankh-Morpork. And the first thing you learn when you enrol at the University is that people don't pay much attention to that kind of thing. It's what their minds tell them that's important.

KELI

You mean people don't see me because their minds tell them not to?

CUTWELL

'Fraid so. It's called predestination, or something. I'm a wizard. I know about these things.

Actually, it's not the first thing you learn when you enrol. I mean, you learn where the lavatories are and that sort of thing before that. But after all that, it's the first thing.

KELI

You can see me though.

CUTWELL

Ah well, wizards are specially trained to see things that are there and not see things that aren't. You get these special exercises . . .

KELI

What can I do?

CUTWELL

Well, you could become a very successful burglar . . . sorry. That was tasteless of me. *(He pats her hand)* You're a lot luckier than most dead people. At least you're alive to enjoy it.

KELI

I don't want to enjoy it!

CUTWELL

You don't understand. History is moving on. There isn't a part for you in it. *(He pats her hand again and stops when she glares)* I know, I'm a wizard. We wizards . . .

KELI

Don't say it! *(she stands)* No. No, I'm not going to accept it. I'm not going to dwindle into some form of ghost. You're going to help me, wizard.

CUTWELL

Me, madam? I don't see what I can . . .

KELI

It's your lucky day, wizard.

CUTWELL

Oh. Good.

KELI

You've just been appointed Royal Recogniser.

CUTWELL

Oh, and what does that entail, exactly?

KELI

You're going to remind everyone that I'm alive. It's very simple. There's three square meals and your laundry done.

CUTWELL

Royal?

KELI
You're a wizard. I think there's something else you should know.

(Lights black out on this scene and come up simultaneously on the next)

SCENE 12 – DEATH'S LIBRARY

(DEATH is sat, reading a sports paper. MORT and YSA-BELL are on stage)

DEATH
  THERE IS? AND WHAT IS THAT? *(pause)* HMM?

MORT
  They – didn't go as smoothly as I thought.

DEATH
  YOU HAD TROUBLE?

MORT
  Well, you see, the witch wouldn't come away, and the monk, well, he started out all over again.

DEATH
  THERE'S NOTHING TO WORRY ABOUT THERE, LAD.

MORT
  Mort.

DEATH
  . . . YOU SHOULD HAVE WORKED OUT BY NOW THAT EVERYONE GETS WHAT THEY

THINK IS COMING TO THEM. IT'S SO MUCH
NEATER THAT WAY.

MORT
I know, sir. But that means bad people who think they're
going to some sort of paradise actually do get there. And
good people who fear they're going to some sort of horrible place really suffer. It doesn't seem like justice.

DEATH
THERE'S NO JUSTICE. THERE'S ONLY ME.
I'VE TOLD YOU THAT.

MORT
Well, I—

DEATH
YOU MUST REMEMBER THAT.

MORT
Yes, but—

DEATH
I EXPECT IT ALL WORKS OUT PROPERLY IN
THE END. I HAVE NEVER MET THE CREATOR,
BUT I'M TOLD HE'S QUITE KINDLY DIS-
POSED TO PEOPLE. PUT SUCH THOUGHTS
OUT OF YOUR MIND. AT LEAST THE THIRD
ONE SHOULDN'T HAVE GIVEN YOU ANY
TROUBLE.

(This is the moment. MORT braces himself, and . . .)

MORT
No, sir.

DEATH
GOOD. WELL DONE. I FEEL INCLINED TO SEE A LITTLE OF LIFE THIS EVENING. YOU CAN TAKE THE DUTY. NOW THAT YOU'VE GOT THE HANG OF IT, AS IT WERE.

MORT *(mournfully)*
Yes, sir.

DEATH
OH YES, ONE MORE THING. ALBERT TELLS ME SOMEONE HAS BEEN MEDDLING IN THE LIBRARY.

MORT
Pardon, sir?

DEATH
TAKING BOOKS OUT, LEAVING THEM LYING AROUND. BOOKS ABOUT YOUNG WOMEN. HE SEEMS TO THINK IT IS AMUSING.

(MORT turns and exchanges a quick glance with YSA-BELL)

MORT
Yes, sir. It won't happen again, sir.

DEATH
>SPLENDID. NOW YOU TWO RUN ALONG. GET
>ALBERT TO DO YOU A PICNIC LUNCH OR
>SOMETHING. GET SOME FRESH AIR. I'VE
>NOTICED THE WAY YOU TWO ALWAYS
>AVOID EACH OTHER. ALBERT'S TOLD ME
>WHAT THAT MEANS.

MORT
>Has he?

(MORT and YSABELL exit as the lights black out)

SCENE 13 – DEATH'S GARDEN, ALMOST
IMMEDIATELY AFTERWARDS

(MORT and YSABELL enter, strolling. We can hear crows cawing in the background. MORT is feeling depressed)

MORT

It's quite a garden, isn't it? Big, black bees buzzing around black hives in the black grass under black–blossomed trees that will – eventually – produce apples that, I wouldn't mind betting, won't be red.

YSABELL

Mort? Why did you let him think it was you in the Library?

MORT

Don't know.

YSABELL

It was . . . very . . . kind of you.

MORT

Was it? I can't think what came over me. *(He hands her her hanky)* This belongs to you, I think. It'd be better if you didn't take the books any more. It upsets them, or something. Ha!

YSABELL

'Ha' what?

MORT

Just Ha!

YSABELL

I was just looking for a bit of company. I didn't want to get married.

MORT

I don't want to get married to anyone, just yet. Certainly not to you. No offence meant.

YSABELL *(sweetly)*

I wouldn't marry you if you were the last boy on the Disc.

MORT

At least I don't look like I've been eating doughnuts in a wardrobe for years.

YSABELL

At least I walk as if my legs only had one knee each.

MORT

My eyes aren't two juugly poached eggs.

YSABELL

On the other hand, my ears don't look like something growing on a dead tree. What does juugly mean?

MORT

You know, eggs like Albert does.

YSABELL

With the white all sticky and runny and full of slimy bits?

MORT

Yes.

YSABELL

A good word. But my hair, I put it to you, doesn't look like something you clean a privy with.

MORT

Certainly, but neither does mine look like a wet hedgehog.

YSABELL

Pray note that my chest does not appear to be a toast rack in a wet paper bag.

MORT

My eyebrows don't look like a pair of mating caterpillars.

YSABELL

True. But my legs, I suggest, could at least stop a pig in a passageway.

MORT

Sorry?

YSABELL
They're not bandy.

MORT
Ah.

YSABELL
Enough?

MORT
Just about.

YSABELL
Good. Obviously we shouldn't get married, if only for the sake of the children.

MORT
Yes.

YSABELL
Are my eyebrows really that bad?

MORT
Um. 'Fraid so.

YSABELL
Oh.

MORT
And my legs?

YSABELL
Yes. Sorry.

MORT
Never mind. At least you can use tweezers.

YSABELL
He's very kind, you know. In a sort of absent-minded way. My real parents were killed crossing the great Nef years ago. There was a storm, I think. He found me and brought me here. I don't know why he did it.

MORT *(sighs)*
I've just upset the entire history of the future.

YSABELL *(not really listening)*
Yes?

MORT
You see, when he tried to kill her, I killed him, but the thing is, according to the history she should have died and the duke would be king, but the worst bit, the worst bit is that although he's absolutely rotten to the core he'd unite the cities and eventually they'll be a federation and the books say there'll be a hundred years of peace and plenty under the duke. But now it's not going to happen and history is flapping around loose and it's all my fault.

YSABELL *(a slight pause)*
You're right, you know. I could use tweezers.

MORT
Did you hear what I said?

YSABELL
What about?

MORT
Oh. Nothing. Nothing much, really.

(Suddenly, and without warning, YSABELL bursts noisily into tears)

Um?

YSABELL
Do you know how old I am?

MORT
Sixteen?

YSABELL
I'm eighteen. And do you know how long I've been eighteen for?

MORT
I'm sorry. I don't under—

YSABELL
No, you wouldn't. No-one would. You haven't been here long enough to notice. Time stands still here, haven't you noticed?
I've been eighteen for thirty-five years.

MORT

  Oh.

YSABELL

It was bad enough the first year.

MORT

Is that why you read all those books?

YSABELL

They're very romantic. There was this girl who drank
poison when her young man died. And another thought
he was dead and she killed herself and then he woke up
and so he did kill himself.

MORT

Doesn't anyone just, you know, get along any more?

YSABELL

To love is to suffer. Did you say something about something flapping about?

MORT

Er, no, no, it's nothing important. Look, er, excuse me,
would you, I've got to go and see a wizard.

(YSABELL sits in her reverie as MORT exits)

YSABELL

So having failed completely to tell me, Albert or Father,
Mort makes his way to Cutwell. Meanwhile history has
split into two separate realities. In the city of Sto Lat,

Princess Keli still rules, with a certain amount of difficulty and with the full-time aid of the Royal Recogniser. But beyond the plain, in the Ramtops, around the Circle Sea and all the way to the Rim, she was quite definitely dead, the duke was king and the world was proceeding sedately according to plan. Whatever that plan is.

People don't alter history any more than birds alter the sky. Inch by inch, implacable as a glacier and far colder, the real reality, like a shimmering but shrinking dome, was grinding back towards Sto Lat.

Logic would have told Mort that here was his salvation. In a day or two the problem would solve itself; the books in Father's library would rewrite themselves; the world would have sprung back into shape like an elastic bandage.

Logic would have told him that interfering with the process a second time around could only make things worse. *Logic* would have said all that . . . if only Logic hadn't taken the night off, too!

(And lights black out)

SCENE 14 – CUTWELL'S FRONT DOOR

(TOWN CRIER enters. Although employed to remind the sleeping populace about the existence of their Queen, he's having trouble with his own memory, too)

TOWN CRIER
Eleven o'clock and all's well! God save our noble Queen, er, Keli! Eleven o'clock and all's well! God save our noble Duke, er Queen, Queen K . . . Ka . . . Keli! All Hail to our most noble Qu, Queen! A long life to him/her, Queen Keli, Keli, yes!

(He exits and we hear his voice fade away as MORT enters and strides masterfully up to the door. On it are several posters declaring KELI to be queen. One of them is over the doorknocker. MORT removes that one)

DOORKNOCKER
Fanks very much. You wouldn't credit it, would you? One minute life as normal, nexft minute a mouthful of glue.

MORT
Where's Cutwell?

DOORKNOCKER
He's gone off to the palace. *(He winks)* Some men came

84

and took his fstuff away. Then some more men came and fstarted pasting up these pictures of his girlfriend all over the place. Barftuds.

MORT
His girlfriend?

DOORKNOCKER
Yeff. They feemed in a bit of a hurry, if you ask me.

(MORT starts to exit)

I fay! I fay! Could you unstick me, boy?

(MORT skids to a halt. He turns and, with his back to the audience, advances on the DOORKNOCKER)

MORT
What – did you call me?

DOORKNOCKER
Fir?

MORT
And what did you ask me to do?

DOORKNOCKER
Unstick me?

MORT
I don't intend to.

DOORKNOCKER
Fine. Fine. That's OK by me. I'll just fstick around then.

(MORT swirls out)

Few! That wav a narrow fsqueak!

(As the door is withdrawn, the lights fade to Ankh–Morpork level. LANDLORD enters)

LANDLORD
· Now come on, sir, it's getting late . . .

(He realises that the person he was talking to has not followed him. He exits and re-enters, ushering DEATH, who is carrying a large floppy Teddy, a plastic bag with a goldfish in it and a tankard which reads 'The Mended Drum, Ankh-Morpork')

DEATH
YOU DRUNK I'M THINK, DON'T YOU?

LANDLORD
I serve anyone who can stand up best out of three.

DEATH
YOU'RE ABSOROOTLY RIGHT. BUT I . . . WHAT WAS I SAYING?

LANDLORD
You said I thought you were drunk.

DEATH

AH, YES, *BUT* I CAN BE SHOBER ANY TIME I LIKE. OH, WHERE'S THE SENSE IN IT? WHAT'S IT REALLY ALL ABOUT?

LANDLORD

Can't say, pal. I expect you'll feel better after a good night's sleep.

DEATH

SLEEP? SLEEP? I NEVER SLEEP. I'M WOSS-NAME . . . PROVERBIAL FOR IT.

LANDLORD

Lucky old you. I do need sleep, though. It's a quarter to three.

DEATH

THERE'S NO-ONE IN THE PLACE BUT YOU AND ME.

LANDLORD *(exiting)*

Yeah, right. Goodnight. Drop in again sometime.

DEATH

THAT'S THE NICESHEST THING . . .

(But the door has slammed in his face. DEATH sobers instantly)

RIGHT. WELL, THAT'S ENOUGH OF THAT, IT'S MAKING MY HEAD ACHE.

(He makes his way to the USL entrance as the revellers enter from the other entrance and start to cross the stage, noisily doing a Conga. As they pass DEATH, each signs for him to join in. The last in the line is a rather tartily dressed WOMAN, dressed in the manner of a Victorian 'lady of the streets')

WOMAN
Why not have a good time, now that you're here?

(She giggles, and DEATH is drawn into the line. He does not know what is expected of him)

Come on, you're not at a funeral, now, dearie! One, two, three – kick!

DEATH
TWO, THREE – KICK? TO KICK VIGOROUSLY IS FUN?

WOMAN
Haven't you ever been to a street carnival before?

DEATH
I'M AFRAID I DON'T GET OUT AS MUCH AS I WOULD LIKE TO. A STREET CARNIVAL IS FUN?

WOMAN
Yes, dearie, lots of things are fun.

DEATH
  THEN THIS IS FUN. WE ARE HAVING FUN.
  WHAT FUN.

*(The revellers have moved off, leaving the WOMAN and
DEATH alone)*

  WHERE'S EVERYBODY GONE? ARE WE STILL
  HAVING FUN?

WOMAN
  You'd better come with me, dearie. Ankh–Morpork's no
  place to be alone after dark.

DEATH
  I WAS JUST SEEING WHAT GOES ON.

WOMAN
  Listen, dearie. There are areas of this city where curios-
  ity not only killed the cat, but threw it into the river with
  weights tied to it.

DEATH
  PEOPLE WHO KILL DUMB ANIMALS . . . NOW
  THAT DOES MAKE ME ANGRY.

WOMAN
  Er . . . yes, dear. You've been to the fair, haven't you?

DEATH
  YOU WANT TO TALK TO ME?

WOMAN
Of course, dearie. I'm a good listener, too.

DEATH
NO-ONE EVER WANTED TO TALK TO ME
BEFORE.

WOMAN
That's a shame.

DEATH
THEY NEVER INVITE ME TO PARTIES, YOU
KNOW.

WOMAN
Tch, tch.

DEATH
THEY ALL HATE ME. I DON'T HAVE A SINGLE
FRIEND.

WOMAN
Well, you've got one now, dearie.

(She indicates DEATH's tankard)

Fancy a quick one?

DEATH
WOULD THAT BE FUN?

WOMAN

That's entirely up to you, dear.

(She puts her arm around his and leads him off, into the Mended Drum, as the Lights Black Out)

SCENE 15 – THE CASTLE OF STO LAT – NIGHT.

(CUTWELL enters, carrying a bowl of strawberries.
Suddenly, MORT bursts in)

CUTWELL
Good grief! The walk-through-walls boy. How did you
get in? The doors are locked and barred.

MORT
Are they? I didn't notice.

CUTWELL
Of course. Are you angry about something? I did start
work for you, but a rather more pressing case came up.

MORT
What are you doing here?

CUTWELL
I could ask you the same thing. Strawberry?

MORT
In mid-winter?

CUTWELL
Actually, they're sprouts with a touch of enchantment.

MORT *(taking one)*
They taste like strawberries?

CUTWELL *(NOTE – if timed right, Mort will have popped in the strawberry just as Cutwell says . . .)*
No. Like sprouts.

MORT *(spitting it out into his hand)*
Why are you here? Is it something to do with all those posters around the town?

CUTWELL
Good idea, wasn't it? My advertising magic, you see. I'm rather pleased with it.

MORT
Look, have you noticed the mist dome around the city?

CUTWELL *(in a panic)*
Already?

MORT
I don't know about already, but there's this sort of crackling wall sliding over the land and no-one else seems to notice it. I saw it on my way over here, it's—

CUTWELL
You saw it? How fast was it moving? How far away was it?

MORT

You were expecting the dome thing, weren't you? What will happen when it closes in?

CUTWELL

I'm not exactly sure. What I think will happen is that the last week will never have existed, the princess will be dead and History will have healed itself. I'm a wizard. We know about these things. Look here.

MORT

What is it?

CUTWELL

It's the Book of the Magick of Alberto Malich the Mage. A sort of book of magical theory. Look, it says here . . . er . . . yes, here we are, it says that even gods—

MORT *(pointing at the book)*

I've seen him before!

CUTWELL

What?

MORT

Him!

CUTWELL

That's not a part of the magic. That's just the author.

MORT

What does it say under the picture?

CUTWELL

Er, it says: 'Yff youe have enjoyed thiss Boke, youe maye be interestede yn othere Titles by—'

MORT

No, no! Right under the picture is what I meant.

CUTWELL

Oh. That's easy. It's old Malich himself. He founded Unseen University. There's a famous statue of him in the quad. Many a student has hung chamber pots on it, or draped it in, erm, foundation garments. One Rag Week I climbed up it and—

MORT

Did he wear gold-rimmed specs and fingerless mitts and have a drip on the end of his nose?

CUTWELL

Dunno.

MORT

When did he live?

CUTWELL

About two thousand years ago, but—

MORT

I bet he didn't die, though. I bet he just disappeared, eh?

CUTWELL
Funny you should say that. They say he blew himself into the Dungeon Dimensions.

MORT
Alberto Malich. Well. Fancy that. I reckon the interface is moving at a slow walking pace. Can't you stop it by magic?

CUTWELL
Not me. It would squash me flat. How far away did you say it was?

MORT
About forty miles.

CUTWELL
That means it will arrive around midnight tomorrow. Oh God. Just in time for Princess Keli's official coronation.

MORT
Where is she? I've got to see her.

(KELI bursts on)

KELI
Aren't the dead allowed any peace? I thought one thing you could be sure of when you were dead was a good night's sleep.

MORT

That's not fair. I've come to help.

KELI

Help? If it wasn't for you . . .

MORT

You'd still be dead. Look, I've got a horse outside. He can take us anywhere. You don't have to wait here.

KELI

Better a dead queen in your own castle than a live commoner somewhere else.

CUTWELL

Wouldn't work, anyway. The dome of reality isn't centred on the palace. It's centred on her.

KELI

On whom?

CUTWELL

On Her Highness.

KELI

Don't you forget it.

MORT

But if you stay here, you'll die.

KELI

Then I shall show the Disc how a queen can die.

MORT

I know how a queen can die. Just like other people. Nothing proud about it. You just die.

KELI

I shall die nobly. Like Queen Ezeriel.

MORT

Who?

CUTWELL

She lived in Klatch and she had a lot of lovers and she sat on a snake.

KELI

She meant to! She was crossed in love!

CUTWELL

All I can remember is that she used to take baths in asses' milk. Funny thing, history. You become a queen, reign for thirty years, make laws, declare war on people and then the only thing you get remembered for is that you smelled of yoghurt and got bitten on the bum.

MORT

Look, this isn't helping the princess. I think I can lay my hands on some powerful magic. Magic will hold back the dome, won't it, Cutwell?

CUTWELL

It would have to be strong stuff. Even then, maybe not. Reality is strong stuff.

MORT

    Right. I shall go. *(melodramatically)* Until tomorrow, farewell! *(exits)*

KELI

    I'm going to get some sleep. Even the dead need some rest. Cutwell, I'm not sure it's wizardly to be alone in a lady's boudoir.

CUTWELL

    Hmm? But I'm not alone, am I? You're here.

KELI

    That, is the point, isn't it?

CUTWELL

    Oh. Yes. Sorry. Goodnight. Um. I'll be seeing you in the morning, then.

KELI

    Goodnight, Cutwell.

(Lights black out)

SCENE 16 – THE JOB CENTRE

(Keeble is sat on stage, fiddling with a card index)

KEEBLE
Next!

(DEATH enters and sits. He hands KEEBLE his application form)

Thank you. And how may I help you?

DEATH
I WOULD LIKE A NEW JOB. PLEASE.

KEEBLE
And what was your previous position?

DEATH
I BEG YOUR PARDON?

KEEBLE
What did you do for a living?

DEATH
I USHERED SOULS INTO THE NEXT WORLD. I
WAS THE ULTIMATE REALITY. I WAS THE

ASSASSIN AGAINST WHOM NO LOCK WOULD
HOLD.

KEEBLE
Yes, point taken, but do you have any particular skills?

DEATH
I SUPPOSE A CERTAIN AMOUNT OF EXPER-
TISE WITH AGRICULTURAL IMPLEMENTS?

(KEEBLE shakes his head)

NO?

KEEBLE
This is a city, Mr . . . Mr . . . Mr . . . Mr . . . , and we're
a bit short of fields. *(He smiles professionally)* My dear
Mr . . . *(looks down at form)* Mr, we get many people
coming into the city from outside because, alas, they
believe life is richer here. Excuse me for saying so, but
you seem to be a gentleman down on his luck. I would
have thought you would have preferred something
rather more refined than . . . *(refers to form)* 'something
nice working with cats or flowers'.

DEATH
I'M SORRY. I THOUGHT IT WAS TIME FOR A
CHANGE.

KEEBLE
Can you play a musical instrument?

DEATH
  NO.

KEEBLE
  Can you do carpentry?

DEATH
  I DO NOT KNOW. I HAVE NEVER TRIED.

(DEATH looks embarrassed. KEEBLE sighs and shuffles his papers)

  I CAN WALK THROUGH WALLS.

KEEBLE *(brightening)*
  I'd like to see that. That could be quite a qualification.

DEATH
  RIGHT. *(stands and walks at the nearest wall)*

  OUCH.

KEEBLE
  Go on, then.

(DEATH feels the wall)

DEATH
  UM. THIS IS AN ORDINARY WALL, IS IT?

KEEBLE
I assume so. I'm not an expert.

DEATH
IT SEEMS TO BE PRESENTING ME WITH
SOME DIFFICULTY.

KEEBLE
So it would appear.

DEATH
WHAT DO YOU CALL THE FEELING OF BEING
VERY SMALL AND HOT?

KEEBLE
Pygmy?

DEATH
IT BEGINS WITH AN M.

KEEBLE
Embarrassed?

DEATH
Yes. I MEAN, YES.

KEEBLE
It would seem that you have no useful talent or skill
whatsoever. Have you thought of going into teaching?
You see, it's very seldom I ever have to find a new career
for an . . . what was it again?

DEATH
  AN ANTHROPOMORPHIC PERSONIFICATION.

KEEBLE
  Oh yes. And what is that, exactly?

DEATH *(rising and striking a pose, with his back to the audience)*
  THIS.

(KEEBLE sees him for the first time. His hands jerk, he utters mumbly sounds and shakes violently. DEATH takes an hourglass from his robe and examines it)

  SETTLE DOWN, YOU'VE GOT A GOOD FEW
  YEARS YET.

KEEBLE
  Bbbbbb . . .

DEATH
  I COULD TELL YOU HOW MANY IF YOU LIKE.

(KEEBLE shakes his head violently)

  DO YOU WANT ME TO GET YOU A GLASS OF
  WATER, THEN?

KEEBLE *(nodding violently)*
  YYYYY . . . yyyyyy . . .

(DEATH produces a glass of water. KEEBLE drinks some)

It's true! I thought you were a nightmare!

DEATH
I COULD TAKE OFFENCE AT THAT.

KEEBLE
You really are Death?

DEATH
YES.

KEEBLE
Why didn't you say?

DEATH
PEOPLE USUALLY PREFER ME NOT TO.

KEEBLE *(a little hysterical)*
You want to do something else? Tooth fairy? Water sprite? Sandman?

DEATH
DO NOT BE FOOLISH. I SIMPLY . . . FEEL I WANT A CHANGE.

(KEEBLE has been riffling through his job cards. He thrusts one at DEATH)

THIS IS A JOB? PEOPLE ARE PAID TO DO THIS? 'SHORT ORDER COOK'?

KEEBLE

Yes. Oh yes. Go and see him, eh? Harga's House of Ribs. You're just the right type. Only don't tell him I sent you.

(DEATH exits and KEEBLE laughs and addresses the audience)

Harga's House of Ribs is the kind of place that doesn't need a menu – you just look at Harga's apron.

So, while Death tries a career change, something is happening back in his library, where he keeps the histories of everyone who has ever lived on the Discworld. The library stack is as dark and silent as a cave deep underground. If you go far enough along the towering shelves, the books run out and there's just clay tablets and lumps of stone and everyone's called Ug and Zog.

Mort and Ysabell have gone to the Stack to try and find the life history of Alberto Malich.

(Black out)

SCENE 17 – DEATH'S OFFICE

(It is dark. MORT and YSABELL enter, carrying books and looking furtive YSABELL is wearing a pink dressing gown with a bunny on it. It is a size too small)

MORT
Right, now we need to . . . what *is* that you're wearing?

YSABELL
Father bought it for me. *(she shrugs)* Why have we got all these?

MORT
We're trying to save someone's life. A princess, as a matter of fact.

YSABELL
A real princess? Can she feel a pea through a dozen mattresses?

MORT
Feel a pea? I thought Albert had got it wrong. We've got Albert's biography. I need a powerful wizard and I think he is one.

YSABELL
Albert?

MORT

Yes. Only he's called Alberto Malich. He's more than two thousand years old, I think. I went to the stack to find his life books. I've got some of them here.

YSABELL

Well, come on, then.

MORT

I must say, you're a real brick.

YSABELL

You mean pink, square and dumpy? You really know how to talk to a girl, my boy.

MORT

Mort. It was hopeless. They didn't seem to be in any order. There were dozens about Albert. A whole shelf. I brought two or three at random.

YSABELL

Pass me one. *(she opens it and reads)* 'was sorelie vexed that alle menne at laste comme to nort, viz. Deathe, and vowed Hymme to seke Immortalitie yn his pride.'

MORT

It's all written in old, before they invented spelling. Let's have a look at the latest one. Yes, look, this is newer, there's references to fried bread and you can hear it writing. Let's see what he's doing now.

YSABELL *(with a giggle)*
'He crept through the dusty darkness, his eyes fixed on the glow of candlelight under the office door. Prying, he thought, poking their noses into things that don't concern them . . .' Mort! He's—

MORT
Let me see . . . 'soon put a stop to this. Albert crept along the corridor. The Master's been acting odd recently, it's all that lad's fault, sooner he's gone the better' *(calling)* Come in, Albert!

ALBERT
Oh. So you've found out, eh? Then much good may it do you. You've no right to go prying.

MORT
I need your help. Something terrible's going to happen.

ALBERT
Terrible things happen all the time, boy.

MORT
Mort.

ALBERT
. . . but no-one expects me to do anything about them. It's no good trying to appeal to my better nature 'cos I ain't got one. Under this crusty exterior my interior's pretty damn crusty, too.

MORT
But you were the greatest.

ALBERT
Forget it. *(to YSABELL)* 'Ere, miss, where's your father?

YSABELL
He's not back.

ALBERT
What? But he's always here. Every morning, working at the nodes. It's his job. He wouldn't miss it.

MORT
I expect the nodes can look after themselves for a day or two.

(ALBERT and YSABELL look at MORT)

They can't?

YSABELL
If the nodes aren't worked out properly, the Balance is destroyed. Anything could happen. Can't you do them?

MORT
We hadn't got on to the theory side yet.

ALBERT
The nodes stop death from getting out of control. I mean, not Death, just dying itself. Death should come

exactly at the end of life, you see, and not before or after . . . They've got to be worked out and the correct hour-glasses got out. But you can't do it?

MORT
No.

ALBERT
Well, that's the whole world in gyppo, then.

MORT
He's probably just got held up somewhere.

ALBERT
Look, Death is not the sort of person people buttonhole to tell him another story, or clap him on the back and say 'You've got time for another half in there, old son'. *(sighs)* Let's have a look at the nodes, then.

(YSABELL gets them. They are large, complex, spirally charts)

MORT
What do they mean?

ALBERT
Sodomy non sapiens.

MORT
What does that mean?

ALBERT
  Means I'm buggered if I know.

MORT
  It's all Klatchian to me. I don't even know if it should be read upside down or sideways.

YSABELL
  Spiralling from the centre outwards.

(They stare at her)

  Father taught me how to read the node chart. When I used to do my sewing in here. He used to read bits out.

MORT
  You can help?

YSABELL
  No.

MORT
  But . . . ?

ALBERT
  What do you mean, no? This is too important for any flighty—

YSABELL
  I mean . . . that I can do them and you can help.

(She settles down. Lights Down. CUTWELL appears in a follow-spot)

CUTWELL
In the meanwhile, Death was hard at work at Harga's House of Ribs, serving up conventional Disc cuisine such as the embryos of flightless birds, minced organs in intestine skins, slices of hog flesh and burnt ground grass seeds dipped in hot animal fats. *(pause)* Egg, sausage, bacon and fried bread to you. Strangely, Death liked working there . . . he was discovering happiness.

(. . . Lights Up. There are now two timers on the desk)

ALBERT
Right. Over to you. The sooner you start, the sooner you'll be finished. I'll go and check Binky.

(ALBERT exits. MORT comes from behind the desk and stalks downstage, walking, just like DEATH himself)

YSABELL
Mort?

MORT *(turning upstage to face her)*
WHAT?

YSABELL
Something's happening to you. You're getting like Father.

MORT
  I KNOW. But I think I can control it.

(*ALBERT re-enters*)

ALBERT
  Right, lad, there's no time to—

(*MORT draws the sword and swings it round to point at ALBERT*)

MORT
  ON YOUR KNEES, ALBERTO MALICH.

ALBERT
  You surely wouldn't dare, boy.

MORT
  MORT.

ALBERT
  There was a pact. There was an agreement.

MORT
  Not with me.

ALBERT
  There was an agreement. Where would we be if we couldn't honour an agreement?

MORT

I don't know where I would be. BUT I KNOW WHERE YOU WOULD GO.

ALBERT

That's not fair!

MORT

THERE'S NO JUSTICE. THERE'S ONLY ME.

YSABELL

Mort! Stop it! You don't really want to kill Albert.

MORT

But I could send him back to the world.

ALBERT

You wouldn't!

MORT

No? I can take you back and leave you there. I shouldn't think you've got much time left, have you? HAVE YOU?

ALBERT

Don't talk like that. You sound like the Master.

MORT *(to YSABELL)*

Pass me Albert's book.

ALBERT

You won't be able to control it forever. You're receptive,

you see? The longer he's away, the more like him you'll become.

(MORT doesn't waver)

They put up a statue to me, you know. And I 'ad me portrait painted. But you don't have a long life as a wizard without making a few enemies. Who'll wait . . . on the Other Side. They ain't all got two legs, either. Some of them ain't got legs at all. Or faces. Death don't frighten me, it's what comes after.

MORT
Help me then. Help me to stop reality from creeping up on Sto Lat castle and killing the princess. I stopped her from being killed last week, you see. But reality's been creeping over the Disc to claim her. I must stop it.

ALBERT
Change reality? You can't. There isn't magic strong enough any more. The Great Spells could've done it. Nothing else. So you might as well do as you please and the best of luck to you.

MORT
You don't get to be a powerful wizard by telling the truth all the time. What does the book say, Ysabell?

ALBERT
You can't believe everything that's writ there!

YSABELL

'he burst out, knowing in his flinty heart that Mort certainly could.'

ALBERT

Stop it!

YSABELL

'he cried, trying to put at the back of his mind the knowledge that even if Reality could not be stopped it could be slowed down a little.'

MORT

HOW?

YSABELL

'intoned Mort in the leaden tones of Death.'

MORT

Yes, yes, we don't need to bother with my bits. Tell me how, wizard.

ALBERT

You don't frighten me, boy.

MORT

LOOK INTO MY FACE AND TELL ME THAT.

YSABELL

'Albert looked into those eyes and the last of his defiance drained away. For he knew that Mort would take him and deliver him to the Dungeon Dimensions where creatures of horror would dot, dot, dot, dot, . . .' It's dots for half a page.

ALBERT
That's because the book daren't mention them.

All right. There is one spell. It slows down time over a little area. I'll write it down, but you'll need to get a wizard to say it.

(He starts writing)

MORT
I can do that.

ALBERT
But you must do the Duty first.

YSABELL
He means it.

MORT
But there isn't time! I'd have to get to Bes Pelargic and back by midnight!

ALBERT
The master would have found time.

MORT
It's a ten thousand mile round trip however you look at it. There's a million to one chance of doing it in time.

ALBERT
When you've been around as long as me, lad, you'll know that million to one chances crop up nine times out of ten. Go to it.

MORT
It can't be done.

YSABELL
I'm sure you'll find a way. And I'll help.

(They exit, leaving ALBERT. He reaches into a hidden cupboard and pulls out a wizard's hat and robe. He puts them on)

ALBERT
Right, my lad. We'll see what the Master's got to say about all this. Now let's have some fun!

(There is a flash, and ALBERT disappears. Lights Out)

SCENE 18 – CASTLE OF STO LAT

(CUTWELL and the HIGH PRIEST are on stage. He is very short-sighted and wears very thick glasses. For much of the time he fails to recognise where on stage Cutwell is, and often addresses the space Cutwell has just vacated)

CUTWELL
Fireworks?

(He moves scross the stage)

HIGH PRIEST *(still speaking to the place CUTWELL left)*
That's the sort of thing you wizard fellows are supposed to be good at, isn't it? Flashes and bangs and whatnot. I remember a wizard when I was a lad . . .

CUTWELL
I'm afraid I don't know anything about fireworks. There's bunting. And I've arranged for the fountain in the town square to run with wine. Well, a reasonable beer made from broccoli, anyway. There'll be folk dancing – at sword point if necessary. The royal coach has been regilded and I'm sure people can be persuaded to notice it as it goes by.

(As soon as he started to speak the HIGH PRIEST moves towards him. As soon as he stops, CUTWELL moves again, leaving the HIGH PRIEST again talking to thin air)

HIGH PRIEST *(still reminiscing)*
Lots of rockets. Thunderflashes. It's not a proper coronation without fireworks.

CUTWELL
Yes, but you see . . .

(Same business)

HIGH PRIEST
Good man. Knew we could rely on you. Plenty of rockets you understand? And to finish with there must be a set piece, something really breathtaking, like a portrait of . . . of . . .

CUTWELL *(wearily)*
The Princess Keli.

HIGH PRIEST
Ah, yes. Her. A portrait of . . . who you said, in fireworks. Of course it's probably all simple stuff to you wizards, but the people like it. See to it. Rockets. With runes on.

(He potters off, colliding with the doorway as he goes)

CUTWELL
Silly old buffer. Still, the populace don't seem to be actually resisting the fact that there'll be a coronation. Mind

you, they're not always clear on who it is who'll be crowned, but still . . .

KELI *(off)*
Is that you, Cutwell?

CUTWELL
Yes.

KELI *(off)*
I'm just getting dressed. I'll be out shortly. *(He rapidly tries to straighten himself up a bit)* Is IT still moving?

CUTWELL
I'm afraid so.

KELI *(off)*
Have we got time?

CUTWELL
I think possibly not. It could be a close run thing.

KELI *(off)*
How close?

CUTWELL
Um. Very.

KELI *(off)*
Are you trying to say it might reach us at the same time as the ceremony?

CUTWELL
Um. More sort of, um, before it.

(KELI enters. She is attractively dressed and CUTWELL makes a slight whinnying noise again)

KELI
How do you know?

CUTWELL
Well, I'm a wiz . . . er, I asked one of the guards about that inn Mort talked about. Then I worked out the approximate distance it had to travel. Mort said it was moving at a slow walking pace, and I reckon his stride is about—

KELI
As simple as that? You didn't use magic?

CUTWELL
Only common sense. Much more reliable in the long run.

KELI
Poor old Cutwell.

CUTWELL
I'm only twenty-three, ma'am. I just hope Mort can come up with something.

KELI

It's hard to have confidence in a ghost. He walks through
walls.

CUTWELL

I've been thinking about that. It's a puzzle, isn't it? He
walks through things only if he doesn't know about it. I
think it's an industrial disease.

KELI

What?

CUTWELL

I was nearly sure last night. He's becoming real.

KELI

But we're all real! At least, you are, and I suppose I am.

CUTWELL

But he's becoming more real. Extremely real. We're the
ones who are less real, that's why he can walk through
things. Extremely real. Nearly as real as Death, and you
don't get much realler. Not much realler at all.

(Lights Black out)

SCENE 19 – THE UNSEEN UNIVERSITY

(There is a flash, and ALBERT is on stage, looking very wizardly)

ALBERT
  Right. I'm back.

(RINCEWIND rushes onto the stage) [NOTE – in fact, we changed this character into just 'a' wizard, feeling it was too much hassle to go to the expense of having a costume made according to the books for a character who is really just incidental to the plot! We called him Stibbons]

RINCEWIND
  Oh, ye gods! *(he glances at the painting, then at ALBERT)*
  Alberto Malich! I think now is a good time, er . . .

(He starts to exit. ALBERT turns and sees him)

ALBERT
  Stop! Come here!

(RINCEWIND does so)

RINCEWIND

All right! All right! I admit it! I was drunk at the time, believe me, I didn't mean it, gosh, I'm sorry, I'm so sorry.

ALBERT

What are you blathering about, man?

RINCEWIND

Your statue, sir . . . it was just high spirits . . . I didn't mean disrespect. I'm so sorry. If I tried to tell you how sorry I am . . .

ALBERT

Stop that bloody nonsense! What's your name, man?

RINCEWIND

Yes, sir, I'll stop, sir, right away, no more nonsense, sir . . . Rincewind, sir. Assistant librarian, if it's all by you.

ALBERT

What sort of librarian would have you for an assistant?

RINCEWIND

An orangutan, sir, if you please, sir.

ALBERT

A monkey! In my university?

RINCEWIND

Orangutan, sir. He used to be a wizard but got caught in some magic, sir, and now he won't let us turn him back, and he's the only one who knows where all the books are. I look after his bananas.

ALBERT
Shut up!

RINCEWIND
Shutting up right away, sir.

ALBERT
And tell me where Death is.

RINCEWIND
Death, sir?

ALBERT
Tall, skeletal, blue eyes, stalks, TALKS LIKE THIS . . . Death. Seen him lately?

RINCEWIND
Not lately, sir.

ALBERT
Well, I want him. This nonsense has got to stop. I'm going to stop it now, see? We're going to summon Death. I want the most senior wizards assembled here in half an hour, with the necessary equipment to perform the Rite of AshkEnte (NOTE – *pronounced ashk-entay*), is that understood? Not that the sight of you gives me any confidence. Bunch of pantywasters, the lot of you.

And now I'm going to the pub. Do they sell any halfway decent cat's piss anywhere these days?

RINCEWIND
There's the Drum, sir.

ALBERT
The Broken Drum? In Filigree Street? Still there?

RINCEWIND
Well, it's been knocked down and rebuilt a few times since your day, sir, and it's called the Mended Drum now, but the site's been on the site for centuries. I guess you're pretty dry after all these years, sir?

ALBERT
What would you know about it?

RINCEWIND
Absolutely nothing, sir.

ALBERT
I'm going to the Drum, then. Half an hour, mind. And if they're not waiting for me when I come back, then, well, they'd just better be.

(He swoops out. RINCEWIND turns to the audience)

RINCEWIND
Well. And I can't even remember walking under a broken mirror.

(Lights black out, clocks chime and the lights come up again to indicate that half an hour has gone past. Now on stage are RINCEWIND and seven other senior wizards, including the BURSAR)

RINCEWIND
   He's coming up the corridor!

ALBERT *(off)*
   Rincewind!

RINCEWIND
   Sir?

(ALBERT enters, carrying a 'frog' (or bat, or whatever you can get))

ALBERT
   Take this thing away and dispose of it. That's the last time that bloody landlord gives any bloody lip to a wizard. It seems I turn my back for a few hundred years and suddenly people in this town are encouraged to think they can talk back to wizards, eh?

BURSAR *(mumbling)*
   Er, well, that is, we—

ALBERT
   What was that? Speak up, that man!

BURSAR

As the bursar of this university I must say that we've always encouraged a good neighbour policy with respect to the community.

ALBERT

Why?

BURSAR

Well, er, a sense of civic duty. We feel it's vitally important that we should show an examp— Aargh!

(There is a flash from ALBERT's fingers and something invisible seems to be choking the BURSAR. [We used a hand-held flash device bought from a magical suppliers] ALBERT walks along the line of wizards)

ALBERT

Anyone else want to show a sense of civic duty? Good neighbours, anybody? You spineless maggots! I didn't found this University so you could lend people the bloody lawnmower!

What's the use of having the power if you don't wield it? Man doesn't show you respect, you don't leave enough of his damned inn to roast a bag of chestnuts! Understand?

WIZARD

But we used to like going into the Drum for a—

ALBERT

Shut up! This is power. This is living. I'll challenge old bonyface and spit in his empty eye. By the Smoking Mirror of Grism, there's going to be some changes round here!

(The BURSAR has absent-mindedly reached for his tobacco pouch and is filling himself a comforting pipe)

What's that man doing?

(The BURSAR hurriedly packs away his stuff)

You there – Rincething! Do yer smoke?

RINCEWIND

No sir! Filthy habit!

(The WIZARDS glare at RINCEWIND, who shrugs apologetically)

ALBERT

Right! Hold my staff. Now you bunch of miserable backsliders, this is going to stop, d'yer hear? First thing tomorrow, up at dawn, three times round the quadrangle and back here for physical jerks! Balanced meals! Study! Healthy exercise! And that bloody monkey goes to a circus!

RINCEWIND

Ape, sir.

ALBERT
   Shut up!!

But first, so that we can summon my old pal, Death, you
will oblige me by setting up the Rite of AshkEnte. I have
some unfinished business.

(Lights Black Out)

SCENE 20 – BES PELARGIC. DINING HALL

(On stage are the PRINCE, the VIZIER, a couple of courtiers and guards. MORT and YSABELL enter)

YSABELL
  Where are we?

MORT
  Bes Pelargic. Agatean Empire.

YSABELL
  Who runs the place?

MORT
  The young emperor, but the top man is really the Grand Vizier. Just don't get in the way. And don't ask questions either.

YSABELL
  Well, no-one seems about to die.

VIZIER
  I am the most unfortunate of mortals, O Imminent Presence, to find such as this in my otherwise satisfactory meal. *(using his chopsticks, he picks up from his plate an odd-shaped morsel)*

PRINCE

The preparer of the food will be disciplined, Noble Personage of Scholarship.

VIZIER

No, O Perceptive Father of your People, I was rather referring to the fact that this is, I believe, the bladder and spleen of the deepwater puff eel, allegedly the most tasty of morsels to the extent that it may be eaten only by those beloved of the gods themselves or so it is written, among such company I do not of course include my miserable self. *(He transfers the morsel to the PRINCE's plate)*

PRINCE

Ah . . . but is it not also written by none other than the great philosopher Ly Tin Wheedle that a scholar may be ranked above princes? I seem to remember you giving me the passage to learn once, O Faithful and Assiduous Seeker of Knowledge. *(using chopsticks, he passes the morsel back)*

VIZIER

Such may generally be the case, O Jade River of Wisdom, but specifically I cannot be ranked above the Emperor whom I love as my own son and have done ever since his late father's unfortunate death, and thus I lay this small offering at your proverbial feet. *(he passes it back)*

MORT

Somebody eat it, for goodness' sake! I'm in a hurry!

PRINCE
Thou art indeed the most thoughtful of servants, O
Devoted and Indeed only Companion of My Late Father
and Grandfather When They Passed Over. And there-
fore I decree that your reward shall be this most rare and
exquisite of morsels. *(and back it goes)*

VIZIER
Alas, it would seem that I have already eaten far too
much . . .

PRINCE
Doubtless it requires a suitable seasoning. *(he nods to the
guard)* My most faithful of servants believes he has no
space left for this fine mouthful. Doubtless you can
investigate his stomach to see if this is true. Take your
knife and . . .

(The VIZIER eats the morsel)

. . . oh, the Vizier seems to be hungry after all. Well done.

*(The VIZIER chews dubiously on the item, and swallows it
with a big gulp)*

VIZIER
Delicious. Superb. Truly the food of the gods, and now,
if you will excuse me . . .

PRINCE
You wish to depart?

VIZIER
  Pressing matters of state, O Perspicacious Personage
  of . . .

PRINCE *(firmly)*
  Be seated. Rising so soon after a meal can be bad for the
  digestion. Besides there are no urgent matters of state
  unless you refer to those in the small red bottle marked
  'Antidote' in the black lacquered cabinet on the bamboo
  rug in your quarters, O Lamp of the Midnight Oil.

(The VIZIER is looking quite poorly)

  You see? Untimely activity on a heavy stomach is con-
  ducive to ill humours. May this message go quickly to all
  corners of my country, that all men may know of your
  unfortunate condition and derive instruction thereby.

VIZIER
  I . . . must . . . congratulate your . . . Personage . . . on
  such . . . consideration. *(and he collapses onto his plate)*

PRINCE
  I had an excellent teacher.

(MORT swings the sword. Strobe effect. The others exit)

MORT
  ABOUT TIME TOO.

YSABELL
  Well! Where now? Back to Sto Lat?

MORT
  STO LAT? STO LAT?

YSABELL
  But I thought you wanted to rescue the princess!

MORT *(shaking his head)*
  I CANNOT. I HAVE NO CHOICE. THERE ARE NO
  CHOICES. I HAVE FINISHED MY APPRENTICE-
  SHIP.

YSABELL
  It's all in your mind! You're whoever you think you are!

(There is a magical, threatening noise. MORT starts to react in pain)

MORT
  SOMEONE IS PERFORMING THE RITE OF ASH-
  KENTE. *(He turns, to walk off)* I COME.

(YSABELL grabs him, to stop him)

  LET ME GO. I HAVE BEEN SUMMONED.

YSABELL
  Not you, you idiot!

MORT
  I COMMAND YOU.

YSABELL

Father tried that tone on me for years. Generally when he wanted me to clean my bedroom. It didn't work then, either.

MORT

THE PAIN . . .

YSABELL

It's all in your mind. You're not Death. You're just Mort. You're whatever I think you are.

(And she hits him. Lights black out)

SCENE 21 – THE UNSEEN UNIVERSITY

*(ALBERT, RINCEWIND and the WIZARDS are gath-
ered around. There is a flash, and DEATH appears, with his
back to the audience. When he turns, we see that he is wearing
a grubby apron bearing the legend 'Harga's House of Ribs'. He
holds a metal spatula in his hand)*

DEATH
  BUGGER. WHY DID YOU HAVE *TO SPOIL IT
  ALL?*

ALBERT
  Spoil it all? Have you seen what that lad has done?

*(DEATH raises his head and sniffs the air. He tears off the
apron)*

DEATH
  IS THIS HOW HE REPAYS MY KINDNESS?
  STEALS MY DAUGHTER, INSULTS MY SER-
  VANT AND RISKS THE FABRIC OF REALITY
  ON A PERSONAL WHIM? I HAVE BEEN FOOL-
  ISH TOO LONG! *(He has grabbed ALBERT by the
  robe)*

ALBERT
  Master, if you would just be so good as to let go of my
  robe.

DEATH
 DID I NOT GIVE HIM THE GREATEST OPPOR-
 TUNITY?

ALBERT
 Exactly, master, and now if you could see your way
 clear—

DEATH
 SKILLS? A CAREER STRUCTURE? A JOB FOR
 LIFE?

ALBERT
 Indeed, and if you would just let go . . . *(to RINCE-
 WIND)* My staff! Throw me my staff! While he is in the
 circle he is not invincible! Let me have my staff and I can
 break free!

RINCEWIND
 Pardon?

DEATH
 OH, MINE IS THE FAULT FOR GIVING IN TO
 THESE WEAKNESSES OF WHAT FOR WANT
 OF A BETTER WORD I SHALL CALL THE
 FLESH.

ALBERT
 My staff, you idiot! My staff!

RINCEWIND
 Sorry?

DEATH
>WELL DONE, MY SERVANT, FOR CALLING ME
>TO MY SENSES. LET US LOSE NO TIME.

ALBERT
>My sta—

(There is an explosion. DEATH and ALBERT disappear)

BURSAR
>That was very unkind, Rincewind, losing his staff like
>that. Remind me to discipline you severely one of these
>days. Anyone got a light?

RINCEWIND
>I don't know what happened to it. I just leaned it against
>a pillar and then . . .

BURSAR
>Well, that was a lesson to us all. I propose that we remove
>the statue of Alberto Malich to a place where it cannot
>be defaced by any more students. And get rid of that
>bloody painting, too.

WIZARD
>Might I suggest we place it in our deepest cellar?

BURSAR
>And lock the door?

RINCEWIND
>And throw away the key?

WIZARD
And weld the door.

BURSAR
And brick up the doorway.

RINCEWIND
And throw away the bricklayer!

BURSAR *(scowling)*
No need to get carried away. Anyone know any spells for turning frogs back into landlords?

(Lights Black out)

SCENE 22 – BES PELARGIC

(MORT is sitting on the ground, with YSABELL by him)

MORT
    Did you hit me?

YSABELL
    Yes.

MORT
    Oh. Thank you.

YSABELL
    Any time. Are we going to rescue this princess of yours?

MORT
    What happened to me?

YSABELL
    Someone used the Rite of AshkEnte. Father hates it, he
    says they always summon him at inconvenient moments.
    The part of you that was Death wanted to go. I stopped
    you. At least you've got your own voice back, now.

MORT
    What time is it?

YSABELL

I don't know.

MORT

It's midnight.

YSABELL

Does that mean we're too late?

MORT

Yes.

YSABELL

I'm sorry. I wish there was something I could do.

MORT

There isn't.

YSABELL

At least you kept your promise to Albert.

MORT *(bitterly)*

Yes. At least I did that. Nearly all the way from one side of the Disc to the other . . . Midnight.

YSABELL

Gone midnight, now.

MORT

Yes, but only midnight here. It's not midnight in Sto Lat yet. Come on, Binky can get us there.

YSABELL
  But how?

MORT
  At the speed of night, of course.

(Lights Black Out. We see Mort and Ysabell on Binky and while this goes on, we have Rincewind's monologue)

SCENE 23 – THE CASTLE OF STO LAT

(RINCEWIND is on stage)

RINCEWIND

So, I never did get that telling off from the Bursar, you know.

Right, now, then, Mort and Ysabell are racing back across the Disc towards Sto Lat, but the interface with Reality is only a street away from the castle. Somewhere outside the dome of the interface, a Cutwell is asleep in his bed and none of this has happened. But another Cutwell is still in the castle, attending a very shortened coronation ceremony . . .

(On stage are CUTWELL, KELI, the DUKE OF STO HELIT, the very short-sighted HIGH PRIEST, an ACOLYTE and guests)

HIGH PRIEST

Hear me, O gods . . . hear me, O Blind Io of the Hundred Eyes; hear me, O Great Offler of the Bird-Haunted Mouth; hear me, O Merciful Fate . . .

CUTWELL *(grabbing the ACOLYTE)*

Stop him! There are over nine hundred known gods on the Disc! We don't have time for all of them!

ACOLYTE

The gods would be displeased.

CUTWELL

Not half as displeased as me – and I'm here!

HIGH PRIEST

Hear me, O Cold, mm, Destiny, hear me, O Seven-Handed Sek; hear me, O Hoki of the Woods; hear me, Steikheigel, god of, mm, isolated cow byres; hear me, O Great and Bounteous . . .

(The ACOLYTE whispers to him)

Hello? What? *(whisper)* This is, mm, very irregular. Very well, we shall go straight to the, mm, Recitation of the Lineage. *(whisper)* Oh, all right. *(scowling at where he thinks CUTWELL is)* Mm, prepare the incense and fragrances for the Shriving of the Fourfold-Path. *(whisper. His face darkens)* I suppose a short prayer is, mm, totally out of the question?

KELI

If some people don't get a move on, there is going to be trouble.

(More whispering at the HIGH PRIEST)

HIGH PRIEST

I don't know, I'm sure. People might as well not bother with a religious, mm, ceremony at all. Fetch the bloody elephant, then.

CUTWELL
    Elephant?

ACOLYTE
    He can't see anything smaller. The last time we used a
    lamb he sacrificed the Bishop of Lancre *(NOTE – pro-
    nounced 'lanker')* by mistake. Er, this way, your
    Reverence.

HIGH PRIEST
    I certainly don't need your help, my lad! I've been sac-
    rificing man and boy – and, mm, women and animals –
    for seventy years, and when, mm, I can't use the knife,
    you put me to bed with a shovel!

KELI
    I think we will dispense with the sacrifice. If someone
    would just fetch the crown.

(STO HELIT produces a crossbow, and steps forward)

STO HELIT
    The wizard will put his hands where I can see them.
    Right, take them away and kill them. Don't put them
    in a cellar with just enough time for the mice to eat
    away the ropes before the floodwaters rise, don't put
    them in a room with a secret passage, don't waste
    time gloating over them, just take them away and kill
    them.

CUTWELL
You won't get away with this. Well, you probably will get away with it, but you'll feel very bad about it on your deathbed and wish you hadn't.

(Magical sound effect. [NOTE – we used some specially created electronic burblings, together with a 'glitter-ball'] CUTWELL has seen the interface coming through the fourth wall)

STO HELIT
What? What is it? What have you seen, wizard?

CUTWELL *(to KELI)*
The interface! It's here, look! *(to STO HELIT)* You won't get away with it. You won't even be here. This is going never to have happened, do you realise?

STO HELIT
Watch his hands. If he so much as moves his fingers, shoot them.

CUTWELL
It doesn't matter if you kill me in here, because tomorrow I'll wake up in my own bed, and—

(MORT and YSABELL burst in)

MORT
Don't you lay a finger on her! I'll have your head off!

STO HELIT *(drawing his sword)*
    This is very impressive. And also very foolish, I—

(But CUTWELL has hit him with a candlestick)

CUTWELL
    Anyone else want some?

(The room empties, leaving just MORT, KELI, YSABELL and CUTWELL. The lighting begins to reduce the acting area until the four are in one lit corner by an exit)

MORT
    Any ideas? I've got the magic spell here somewhere . . .

CUTWELL
    Forget it, the dome of Reality's too small, now. If I try any magic in here it'll blow our heads off.

KELI
    Am I going to be crowned or not? I've got to die a queen. It'd be terrible to be dead and common!

YSABELL
    Is this it?

KELI
    That's the crown. But there's no priest or anything.

MORT
    Cutwell, if this is our own reality we can arrange it the way we want, can't we?

CUTWELL
What do you mean?

MORT
You're a priest now. Name your own god.

KELI
You're all making fun of me!

MORT
Sorry, it's been a long day.

CUTWELL
I hope I can do this right. I've never crowned anyone before.

KELI
I've never been crowned before. We can learn together.

CUTWELL *(placing the crown on her head and chanting in mock CofE style)*
I-play-better-dominoes-than-you-do. Now, any ideas about escape?

MORT
Yes. We can go home.

CUTWELL
What?

YSABELL
To my father's country. Come on, Binky can take us all out before the interface closes.

CUTWELL
Binky?

YSABELL
My father's flying horse.

CUTWELL
Erm . . . your father?

YSABELL
Death

CUTWELL
Oh. Great.

(Lights Black Out. We see Binky carrying the heavy load of Mort, Ysabell, Cutwell and Keli through the sky back to Death's house)

SCENE 24 – DEATH'S STUDY

(YSABELL, MORT, CUTWELL and KELI enter, quietly)

YSABELL
There's no-one at home. You'd better come in.

MORT
Have you looked everywhere?

YSABELL
I can't even find Albert. Would anyone like a drink? *(They all ignore this)* What are we going to do now? Father will be very angry if he finds them here.

MORT
I'll think of something. I'll rewrite the autobiographies or something. I'll think of something.

(DEATH and ALBERT are revealed on stage)

DEATH
YOU HAD BETTER START NOW. DON'T BOTHER TO APOLOGISE. I AM BACK. AND I AM ANGRY.

MORT
  Master, I . . .

DEATH
  SHUT UP. *(He beckons KELI to him and touches her
  chin)* IS THIS THE FACE THAT LAUNCHED A
  THOUSAND SHIPS AND BURNED THE TOP-
  LESS TOWERS OF PSEUDOPOLIS?

CUTWELL
  Er, excuse me.

DEATH
  WELL?

CUTWELL
  It isn't, sir. You must be thinking about another face.

DEATH
  WHAT IS YOUR NAME?

CUTWELL
  Cutwell, sir. I'm a wizard, sir.

DEATH
  I'M A WIZARD, SIR. BE SILENT, WIZARD.

CUTWELL
  Sir.

DEATH *(to YSABELL)*
DAUGHTER, EXPLAIN YOURSELF. WHY DID
YOU AID THIS FOOL?

YSABELL
I . . . I love him, Father. I think.

MORT
You do? You never said.

YSABELL
There didn't seem to be time. Father, he didn't mean—

DEATH
BE SILENT.

YSABELL
Yes, father.

*(DEATH stalks round to MORT. Suddenly, in slow motion,
with the strobe, he slaps MORT across the face)*

DEATH
I INVITE YOU INTO MY HOME. I TRAIN YOU. I
FEED YOU. I CLOTHE YOU, I GIVE YOU
OPPORTUNITIES YOU COULD NOT EVEN
DREAM OF, AND THUS YOU REPAY ME. YOU
NEGLECT THE DUTY, YOU MAKE RIPPLES IN
REALITY THAT WILL TAKE A CENTURY TO
HEAL. YOUR ILL-TIMED ACTIONS HAVE
DOOMED YOUR COLLEAGUES TO OBLIVION.
THE GODS WILL DEMAND NOTHING LESS.

ALL IN ALL, BOY, NOT A GOOD START TO
YOUR FIRST JOB.

MORT
Mort!

DEATH
IT SPEAKS! WHAT DOES IT SAY?

MORT
You could let them go. They just got involved. It wasn't
their fault. You could rearrange this so . . .

DEATH
WHY SHOULD I DO THAT? THEY BELONG TO
ME NOW.

MORT
I'll fight you for them.

DEATH
AH, A CHALLENGE, EH?

MORT
And if I win . . .

DEATH
IF YOU WIN, YOU WILL BE IN A POSITION TO
DO AS YOU CHOOSE.

CUTWELL
Are you sure you know what you're doing?

MORT
  No.

ALBERT
  You can't beat the master. Take it from me.

KELI
  And what will happen if you lose?

MORT
  I won't lose. That's the problem.

YSABELL
  Father wants him to win.

CUTWELL
  You mean he'll let Mort win?

YSABELL
  Oh no, he won't let him win. He just wants him to win.
  He wants to stop being Death, I think.

CUTWELL *(picking up an hourglass)* *[NOTE – this was
a trick hourglass designed to break at the appropriate
moment in the fight]*

  Whose is this one?

ALBERT *(sharply)*
 Put that down! That's the Duke of Sto Helit. I've just
 been scraping some corrosion off his bottom.

(CUTWELL replaces it on the table)

DEATH
 ALBERT, FETCH THE GLASSES.

ALBERT
 Yes, master.

CUTWELL
 You're a wizard! You don't have to do what he says!

ALBERT
 When you're my age, lad, you'll see things differently.
 Sorry.

*(MORT and DEATH prepare. ALBERT returns with the
glasses. DEATH's has no sand in it)*

YSABELL
 But that's not fair! Mort's sand's almost run out, and
 your glass has none in at all!

DEATH
 MR WIZARD, SIR, YOU WILL BE SO KIND AS
 TO GIVE US A COUNT OF THREE.

CUTWELL
 Are you sure this couldn't be sorted out by just getting
 round a table—

MORT/DEATH
  NO.

CUTWELL
  One . . . Two . . .

(and they start fighting. Slow motion. Strobe effect)

KELI
  They both cheated!

YSABELL
  Of course.

(As they fight, the DUKE's hourglass is knocked off the desk or shelf and breaks on the ground)

  The Duke of Sto Helit!

KELI
  Isn't there something we can do?

YSABELL
  Mort will lose either way.

(MORT shows signs of tiredness)

DEATH
  YIELD, I MAY BE MERCIFUL. THUS IT ENDS, BOY.

MORT
  Mort. Mort. Mort, you bastard!

(MORT flies at DEATH in a fury, and DEATH is driven back against a wall. He holds the scythe away from himself)

DEATH
  STRIKE.

(A pause)

MORT
  No.

(MORT lowers the sword. DEATH lashes out with the scythe handle at groin height and MORT doubles up. DEATH hands the scythe to ALBERT, grabs Mort's hourglass and advances on MORT, holding it aloft, ready to smash it. YSABELL comes in front of him)

YSABELL
  You're right. There's no justice. There's just you.

DEATH
  YOUR MEANING?

(YSABELL slaps him)

  WHY?

YSABELL
You said that to tinker with the fate of one individual could destroy the whole world.

DEATH
YES?

YSABELL
You meddled with his. And mine. And *(indicating the broken glass)* with the now late Duke of Sto Helit.

DEATH
WELL?

YSABELL
What will the gods demand for that?

DEATH
FROM ME? THE GODS CAN DEMAND NOTHING OF ME. EVEN GODS ANSWER TO ME, EVENTUALLY.

YSABELL
Doesn't seem very fair, does it? Don't the gods bother about justice and mercy?

DEATH
I APPLAUD YOUR EFFORTS, BUT THEY AVAIL YOU NAUGHT. STAND ASIDE.

YSABELL
No.

DEATH
YOU MUST KNOW THAT EVEN LOVE IS NO
DEFENCE AGAINST ME. I AM SORRY. I CAN-
NOT BE BIDDEN. I CANNOT BE FORCED. I
WILL DO ONLY THAT WHICH I KNOW TO BE
RIGHT.

*(He gestures and YSABELL is forced out of the way, by some
unseen power)*

YOU DON'T KNOW HOW SORRY THIS MAKES
ME.

MORT
I might.

*(A pause. Then DEATH starts to laugh. We hear the roar of
sand in MORT's hourglass. Death's laugh echoes and re-
echoes. [NOTE – we used Death's live laugh on stage,
supplemented by a recording of his laugh, overlapping and
building to a climax] Then he turns MORT's hourglass over.
Black out)*

SCENE 25 – CASTLE OF STO LAT

(MORT, YSABELL etc. on stage, plus guests, MC etc.)

MC
The Royal Recogniser, Master of the Queen's Bed–
chamber, His Ipississumussness Igneous Cutwell,
Wizard first grade.

(Enter CUTWELL, finely robed)

CUTWELL
May I kiss the bride?

YSABELL
If it's allowed for wizards.

MORT
We thought the fireworks were marvellous. I expect
they'll soon be able to rebuild the outer wall.

YSABELL
They say you're the real power behind the throne now–
adays.

CUTWELL
Shutuphereshecomes.

MC

Her Supreme Majesty, Queen Kelirehenna I, Lord of Sto Lat, Protector of the Eight Protectorates and Empress of the Long Thin Debated Piece Hubwards of Sto Kerrig.

KELI

How's Sto Helit?

MORT

Fine, fine. We'll have to do something about the cellars, though, the Duke had some rather odd hobbies.

YSABELL

She means you, you nit. That's your official name now that you're the Duke.

MORT

I preferred Mort.

KELI

Such an interesting coat of arms, too. Crossed scythes on an hourglass rampant against a sable field. It gave the Royal College quite a headache.

MORT

I don't mind being a duke. It's being married to a duchess I find difficult.

KELI
You'll get used to it. Now, Ysabell, if you are to move in royal circles, there are some people you simply must meet. Cutwell!

(They move away from MORT)

MC
The Stealer of Souls, Defeater of Empires, Swallower of Oceans, Thief of Years, The Ultimate Reality, Harvester of Mankind, the—

DEATH
ALL RIGHT. ALL RIGHT. I CAN SEE MYSELF IN.

MORT
We didn't think you'd come.

DEATH
TO MY OWN DAUGHTER'S WEDDING? ANYWAY IT WAS THE FIRST TIME I'VE EVER HAD AN INVITATION TO ANYTHING. IT HAD GOLD EDGES AND RSVP AND EVERYTHING.

MORT
Yes, but when you weren't at the service . . .

DEATH
I THOUGHT PERHAPS IT WOULD NOT BE ENTIRELY APPROPRIATE.

MORT

Well, yes, I suppose so . . .

DEATH

I HAVE DECIDED NOT TO INTEREST MYSELF
IN HUMAN AFFAIRS ANY FURTHER.

MORT

Really?

DEATH

EXCEPT OFFICIALLY, OF COURSE. IT WAS
CLOUDING MY JUDGEMENT.

MORT

What happened? I've got to know! Reality was altered to
fit us in. Who did it?

DEATH

I HAD A WORD WITH THE GODS.

MORT

I shouldn't think they were very pleased.

DEATH

THE GODS ARE JUST. THEY ARE ALSO SENTI-
MENTALISTS. I HAVE NEVER BEEN ABLE TO
MASTER IT, MYSELF. BUT YOU AREN'T FREE
YET. YOU MUST SEE TO IT THAT HISTORY
TAKES PLACE.

MORT
I know. Uniting the kingdoms and everything.

DEATH
YOU MIGHT END UP WISHING YOU HAD
STAYED WITH ME.

MORT
I certainly learned a lot. But I don't think I was cut out
for that sort of work. Sorry. Thanks for the toast rack,
by the way.

DEATH
THERE WAS ANOTHER THING. *(He takes out a
gift-wrapped book)* IT'S FOR YOU. PERSONALLY.
YOUR BOOK.

MORT
There's a lot of pages left to fill. How much sand have I
got left, now that you've turned the glass over? Because
Ysabell said that . . .

DEATH
YOU HAVE SUFFICIENT. MATHEMATICS
ISN'T ALL IT'S CUT OUT TO BE.

MORT
How do you feel about being invited to christenings?

DEATH
  ON THE WHOLE, I THINK NOT. I WASN'T CUT
  OUT TO BE A GRANDFATHER. I HAVEN'T
  GOT THE RIGHT KIND OF KNEES.

  MY REGARDS TO YOUR GOOD LADY. NOW I
  REALLY MUST BE OFF. DUTY CALLS. YOU
  KNOW HOW IT IS.

(They shake hands)

MORT
  Look, if ever you want a few days off, you know, if you'd
  like a holiday . . .

DEATH
  MANY THANKS FOR THE OFFER. I SHALL
  THINK ABOUT IT MOST SERIOUSLY. AND
  NOW . . .

MORT
  Goodbye. It's such an unpleasant word, isn't it?

DEATH
  QUITE SO.

  I PREFER AU REVOIR.

(Black Out)

THE END

MORT – PROPS LIST

On the furniture side, we had one desk and two chairs that were dressed variously for Death's study, Cutwell's and Keeble's, a 'bookshelf and books' for the library, a door with a hole in it (for the Doorknocker's head!) and a tall pedestal with a flat top (Alberto Malich's book, Sto Helit's hourglass, etc.)

Property	Scene Where First Used	Used By
Tray of Sausages (or the like)	I	Trader
Scythe	I	DEATH
Sword	I	DEATH
Purse of Coins	I	DEATH
Large Books and Hourglasses	2	On Stage
Frying Pan with Eggs	2	Albert
Large Book	2	DEATH
Atlas	3	DEATH
Small Bell	3	On Stage
Trays of Drinks	4	Servants
Drinks	4	Courtiers
Hourglass	4	DEATH

Pan and Scourer	4	Albert
Bag of Coins	5	DEATH
Large Handbell	6	Towncrier
Card (Sign)	6	Cutwell's Door
Bag of Chips	6	DEATH
Three Hourglasses (in bag?)	6	DEATH
Bag of Hay	7	On Stage
Sword	9	Assassin
Lighted Candle	9	Keli
Lighted Candle	10	Mort
Large Books	10	Mort
Lace Hanky	10	In Wings
Clutter	11	Cutwell's Hse
Slice of Pizza	11	Cutwell's Hat
Caroc Deck (rigged)	11	On Stage
Magnifying Glass	11	On Stage
Protractors and Ruler	11	On Stage
Newspaper (Discworld)	12	DEATH
Posters ('Long Live Queen Keli', etc.)	14	On Stage
Large Floppy Teddy	14	DEATH
Plastic Bag with 'Goldfish'	14	DEATH
Tankard	14	DEATH
Bowl of Strawberries	15	Cutwell

A LIST OF OTHER TERRY PRATCHETT
TITLES AVAILABLE FROM CORGI BOOKS

THE PRICES SHOWN BELOW WERE CORRECT AT THE TIME OF GOING TO PRESS. HOWEVER TRANSWORLD PUBLISHERS RESERVE THE RIGHT TO SHOW NEW RETAIL PRICES ON COVERS WHICH MAY DIFFER FROM THOSE PREVIOUSLY ADVERTISED IN THE TEXT OR ELSEWHERE.

12475 3	THE COLOUR OF MAGIC	£4.99
12848 1	THE LIGHT FANTASTIC	£4.99
13105 9	EQUAL RITES	£4.99
13106 7	MORT	£4.99
13107 5	SOURCERY	£4.99
13460 0	WYRD SISTERS	£4.99
13461 9	PYRAMIDS	£4.99
13462 7	GUARDS! GUARDS!	£4.99
13463 5	MOVING PICTURES	£4.99
13464 3	REAPER MAN	£4.99
13465 1	WITCHES ABROAD	£4.99
13890 8	SMALL GODS	£4.99
13891 6	LORDS AND LADIES	£4.99
14028 7	MEN AT ARMS	£4.99
14029 5	SOUL MUSIC	£4.99
14235 2	INTERESTING TIMES	£4.99
14161 5	THE STREETS OF ANKH-MORPORK (with Stephen Briggs)	£5.99
14324 3	THE DISCWORLD MAPP (with Stephen Briggs)	£5.99
14430 4	WYRD SISTERS – THE PLAY (adapted by Stephen Briggs)	£4.99
13945 9	THE COLOUR OF MAGIC – GRAPHIC NOVEL	£8.99
14159 3	THE LIGHT FANTASTIC – GRAPHIC NOVEL	£7.99
13325 6	STRATA	£4.99
13326 4	THE DARK SIDE OF THE SUN	£3.99
13703 0	GOOD OMENS (with Neil Gaiman)	£4.99
52595 2	TRUCKERS	£3.99
52586 3	DIGGERS	£3.99
52649 5	WINGS	£3.99
52752 1	THE CARPET PEOPLE	£3.99
13926 2	ONLY YOU CAN SAVE MANKIND	£3.99
52740 8	JOHNNY AND THE DEAD	£3.99
52968 0	JOHNNY AND THE BOMB	£3.99
14005 8	TRUCKERS – AUDIO	£7.99*
14006 6	DIGGERS – AUDIO	£7.99*
14007 4	WINGS – AUDIO	£7.99*
14008 2	ONLY YOU CAN SAVE MANKIND – AUDIO	£7.99*
14033 3	JOHNNY AND THE DEAD – AUDIO	£7.99*
14458 4	JOHNNY AND THE BOMB – AUDIO	£7.99*
14017 1	THE COLOUR OF MAGIC – AUDIO	£7.99*
14018 X	THE LIGHT FANTASTIC – AUDIO	£7.99*
14016 3	EQUAL RITES – AUDIO	£7.99*
14015 5	MORT – AUDIO	£7.99*
14011 2	SOURCERY – AUDIO	£7.99*
14014 7	WYRD SISTERS – AUDIO	£7.99*
14013 9	PYRAMIDS – AUDIO	£7.99*
14012 0	GUARDS! GUARDS! – AUDIO	£7.99*
14010 4	MOVING PICTURES – AUDIO	£7.99*
14415 0	WITCHES ABROAD – AUDIO	£7.99*
14416 9	SMALL GODS – AUDIO	£7.99*

* including VAT